Nobody's Child

To my dear friend
Lee Ann Krekorian-Chan.

NOBODY'S CHILD

Marsha Forchuk Skrypuch

A BOARDWALK BOOK
A MEMBER OF THE DUNDURN GROUP
TORONTO

Editor: Barry Jowett
Copy-Editor: Jennifer Bergeron
Design: Jennifer Scott
Printer: Webcom

National Library of Canada Cataloguing in Publication Data

Skrypuch, Marsha Forchuk, 1954-
  Nobody's child / Marsha Forchuk Skrypuch.

ISBN 1-55002-442-6

1. Armenian massacres, 1915-1923 — Juvenile fiction. 2. Death marches — Juvenile fiction. I. Title.

PS8587.K79N63 2003   jC813'.54   C2003-905439-X

  2   3   4   5   07   06   05   04

We acknowledge the support of the **Canada Council for the Arts** and the **Ontario Arts Council** for our publishing program. We also acknowledge the financial support of the **Government of Canada** through the **Book Publishing Industry Development Program** and **The Association for the Export of Canadian Books**, and the **Government of Ontario** through the **Ontario Book Publishers Tax Credit** program, and the **Ontario Media Development Corporation's Ontario Book Initiative.**

Care has been taken to trace the ownership of copyright material used in this book. The author and the publisher welcome any information enabling them to rectify any references or credits in subsequent editions.

J. Kirk Howard, President

Printed and bound in Canada.
Printed on recycled paper.

www.dundurn.com

Dundurn Press
8 Market Street
Suite 200
Toronto, Ontario, Canada
M5E 1M6

Gazelle Book Services Limited
White Cross Mills
Hightown, Lancaster, England
LA1 4X5

Dundurn Press
2250 Military Road
Tonawanda, NY
U.S.A. 14150

BOOK ONE

CHAPTER ONE

April 1909 — Adana, Turkey

They travelled on foot. That set them apart from the other migrant barley harvesters. The others travelled with donkeys or an oxcart. What also set them apart was that their group included women and children.

Mariam's father and uncle kept pace a few steps in front of the others in their group, and right behind them walked Mariam's mother. They each carried a cloth sack of supplies on their backs. They each brought their own large sickle.

As Mariam put one foot in front of the other, she kept her eyes fixed on the small glittering sickle looped into the left side of her mother's belt. Mariam Hovsepian didn't like to think that her mother, Parantzim, was only fifteen years older than she was. Would she look that old at twenty-five? Mariam closed her eyes for a second and then opened them again. The edge of her mother's coarsely woven wool skirt was stiff with dirt from the road and there was a patch of sweat on her back. The gauzy veil that she wore to keep the sun off her head and face kept slipping off, and several times Mariam reached down and picked it up off the dirt and handed it back to her mother.

Onnig, Mariam's four-year-old brother, was riding on Parantzim's right hip. The sway of the movement had lulled him to sleep for most of the day, but now he struggled to get down. Parantzim held him firmly but gently in place and cooed in his ear. Mariam knew that her mother did not want to slow the group down by letting him walk.

Beside Mariam walked Marta, her little sister. She was seven years old, but tall for her age. Marta was built sturdily, and she wore her unruly hair tied back with a strip of leather. On Marta's hip was balanced Bibi — her beloved rag-cloth doll.

"Are we there yet?" asked Onnig wearily.

This was their sixth day of travel. They had already stopped at several farms along the way, but nobody had wanted to hire a whole family of field hands.

"I told you we should have left them at home, Hovsep," Aram said, in a voice filled with annoyance.

Mariam understood why her father's older brother was upset. Last April, her father and uncle had been able to find good paying jobs in the barley fields within a single day of leaving Marash. And here they were now — so close to Adana that its distinctive stone bridge across the Jihan River could be seen in the distance.

And still not an offer.

What was her mother thinking, dragging the whole family on this journey with the men? She and her brother and sister would have been much better off staying at home with their extended family. And her mother should have stayed at home too.

But while she agreed with her uncle Aram, Mariam also understood why her mother insisted on coming with her husband. And also why she wanted to bring the children. Parantzim had heard rumours of political unrest. There was talk that the Armenian district in Marash was going to be raided while the men were gone for the harvest.

"Parantzim and your children should have stayed at home with our mother and my wife and children," said Aram.

"We've been over this a thousand times, brother. What's done is done."

The conversation drifted back to Parantzim, and Mariam could see that her mother's ears burned pink in shame.

As the little group reached a narrow dirt laneway of another farm, Hovsep said wearily, "Wife, children, rest here while Aram and I see if there is work to be had in these fields."

Gratefully, Mariam sat down in a patch of dry grass and pulled the leather strapped sandals off her feet and gingerly rubbed the blister that had formed at the back of her heel. Marta plopped down beside her, and Onnig struggled down from his mother's hip, full of energy and ready to play. Parantzim dug a water skin from the folds of her robe and sat down beside her children.

"Water, please?" asked Onnig, opening his mouth expectantly. So Parantzim squeezed a thin spray of tepid water into his mouth. Then she gave the skin to Mariam, then Marta, and then finally took a sip of water herself.

They had barely settled down when Hovsep came running down to them. "There is work for us here, even for you, Parantzim," he said excitedly. "The boss is showing Aram where we can set up camp."

The accommodation was little more than a barn. And when the girls and their mother stepped inside, they were welcomed with rude sexual hoots and guffaws from the other migrant workers. Mariam looked over at her mother and noticed that her expression was frozen into a mask of indifference. With forced dignity, Parantzim turned to her husband and addressed him formally. "We will sleep under the stars, Hovsep-agha. It's too filthy in here for humans." And she turned her back on the loud catcalls and stinking humanity.

Her sister rolled out a carpet on one side of Onnig and Mariam rolled hers out on the other. Aram collected some twigs and brush to make a fire, and Hovsep drew water from a nearby well. Parantzim broke into their thin store of food yet another time. She filled a pot with water and threw in a cupful of dried wheat berries. She rooted around in the food bag and found an onion. She peeled it and added it to the pot.

While the pilaf cooked, Parantzim untied the large cloth that held a stack of dried Armenian flatbread. She removed two platter-sized pieces of the bread, then tied the cloth back up. She shook out another cloth, spread it onto one of the carpets beside the fire, and placed on it the flatbreads side by side. She squirted some water onto each piece of bread and then quickly distributed the droplets of water evenly over the surface with the palms of her hands. Within minutes, the bread was moist and fresh and ready to eat. She knew her family was too hungry to wait the hour it would take for the pilaf to cook, so she took out what was left of a salted roast of lamb, cut a few slices, and set it out.

While the pilaf cooked, Parantzim ripped off bits of flatbread and wrapped each one around a slice of salted lamb. She gave one small wrapped sandwich to each family member to stave off hunger pangs until the pilaf was ready.

Mariam's wrap was finished in two quick bites. She was so tired that she didn't think she'd be able to stay awake long enough for dinner, but as the pilaf cooked, the savoury aroma bubbling out of the pot made her stomach grumble.

Everyone received a piece of flatbread and they ate the pilaf family style, each breaking off bite-sized pieces of the bread and dipping it into the communal pot. Mariam dipped every last piece of her bread into the pot, savouring each bite. She was fast asleep moments after finishing.

She dreamed of a soft bed and food to eat and servants to cater to her every need. What a grand life that would be. But when the sun beat down on her in the early hours of the morning, she opened her eyes and found that she was still just the daughter of a lowly migrant worker.

In the morning, Mariam awoke to the aroma of fresh coffee. Her mother had lit a fire just big enough to boil a bit of water in the long-handled pot and then threw in a handful of freshly ground beans.

"You're old enough now," said Parantzim, handing her oldest daughter a chipped demitasse cup of the rich dark brew.

Mariam nodded gravely, then breathed in the heady aroma before taking her first sip.

Parantzim gave Onnig and Marta each a piece of flatbread and a dried apricot and they ate quickly, quenching their thirst from a stream nearby.

Mariam savoured her coffee to the last dregs, then she did what her mother always did: she turned the demitasse upside down in the saucer and gave it half a turn. Parantzim sat down beside her oldest daughter, balancing her own demitasse of coffee. She regarded Mariam's inverted cup resting on the ground beside her.

"Would you like me to tell your fortune?"

Mariam's eyes sparkled. "Yes," she said. And she handed her mother her cup.

Parantzim placed the pad of her index finger on the bottom of the upturned cup. "It's cool enough now," she said. She turned the cup right side up and peered inside.

Mariam looked in too.

The coffee grounds had made a pattern of black-brown rivulets down the side of the cup. Parantzim pointed to a splotch just below the cup handle. "That's you," she said.

Mariam nodded.

"You are surrounded by people who love you."

Mariam smiled. She knew that.

Parantzim frowned. "They all love you," she said, "but the people on your left love you for your good heart, while the people on your right love you for ... I can't make it out."

Mariam looked at her mother. "What do you mean?"

"I don't know," said Parantzim, frowning. "There is much love. Yet ..." She set down the cup. "This is all nonsense, anyway," she said. "I never believe the coffee grounds."

Parantzim finished her own coffee, and Mariam noticed that she didn't invert her cup. Her mother stood up, then brushed stray bits of dust from her gown. "It is time to go to the fields," she said. "Keep an eye on Onnig and Marta."

Then she and Hovsep and Aram gathered their tools and walked towards the fields.

Mariam liked to pretend that she was Onnig's mother, so she balanced him on her hip. Marta balanced her doll on her own hip and then the two sisters wandered away from the campsite to pick the colourful spring anemones that grew so abundantly under the wild olive trees that dotted the meadows. Mariam was amazed by the vast variety of spring flowers. Being a city girl from Marash, she was used to cultivated flowers, but not these lush wild ones in every imaginable colour. She made a long chain of giant daisy-like pale mauve flowers and draped it around Marta's neck. Marta grinned with pleasure at the adornment.

"Let's explore further," Mariam suggested.

In the distant horizon, they could see a strip of deep blue sea and the outline of an ancient Crusader castle. The sight took Mariam's breath away. She had heard tales of the Crusaders since she was little. What must it have been like to live in such a splendid place so many centuries ago?

"I want to go there," said Onnig, pointing to the castle.

"It's much further than it looks," replied Mariam.

Not too far from the flower-covered meadow was a barren rocky area close to the farmer's fields, and the children were drawn there. They found a series of shallow caves and even more patches of spring flowers and fragrant wild grasses. Onnig was restless, so Mariam let him down from her hip.

While Adana itself was miles away, when Mariam stood on one of the big rocks she could see a patch or two of flowering bushes, and if she breathed in deeply, she could catch the faint spicy scent of mulberry blossoms. This area was known for its cultivated mulberry trees. She had never tasted the berries, which were reserved for the precious silk worms. The scent was marvellous enough.

She shielded her eyes from the sun and looked in another direction. There was a small village within easy walking distance. Perhaps there were other children down there, she thought. Maybe they'd be able to find someone Onnig's age and they could play together. With her eyes, Mariam motioned to her sister.

"As long as we avoid the Turkish quarters, we should be all right," Mariam reasoned.

The children had learned early to always avoid the Turkish area of any village or city. It was common knowledge that Turks considered Armenians barely human, and retribution came swiftly to Armenians who got out of line. Mariam had never questioned this attitude. It was a fact of life.

The trio headed down.

The first thing they saw when they stepped through the stone gates was a haphazard row of clay one-storey homes that looked just like those in their own neighbourhood in Marash. Each home had a flat roof that doubled as a terrace, and each had a walled-in fruit and vegetable garden where a goat or a few chickens could run free. Just as in their own neighbourhood, the streets were narrow and maze-like, with dead ends and twisty turns. Mariam saw a photograph in a book once of a street in London. It amazed her that the houses were lined up uniformly along either side of a wide paved street. The strangest thing about the foreign English houses was that they were so far away from each other that you would never be able to walk from roof to roof. In virtually any town Mariam had ever been to, it was possible to travel blocks without ever setting foot on the ground. That's probably why they have wide streets, mused Mariam. They needed them for all their walking. Some day she would love to travel to London and see that strange city for herself!

The children walked through the maze of streets, backtracking several times when they reached a dead end. Then, suddenly, the street they were on opened up to a wide square. There was a communal well, the church, and open-air stores. Several wives gossiped by the well, while husbands watched two elderly men play a board game of dama under the shade of a tree.

Mariam knew it was the Armenian section right away because there were many women out in public, and the bottom half of their faces weren't covered with veils.

Mariam could hear the shrieks of children playing. She squinted her eyes from the sun so she could see beyond the well, and saw that a game of "Turks and Armenians" was in progress.

"Look, Onnig," she said, lifting him up so he could see better. "Would that be fun?"

Onnig grinned. "I want to play." He struggled down from her arms, then grabbed one of her hands and one of Marta's. "Come on," he said excitedly, pulling his sisters towards the other children.

Mariam smiled as she watched two children play the familiar game. It could involve two or twenty children, as long as there were enough for two teams. No one ever wanted to be the Turks, however, and so straws would have to be drawn. Then the children would make a pile of stones in the middle of the play area. This was the "fortress." And then each team fought for possession of the fortress. The children on the Turks side would call their opponents "infidels" and the children on the Armenian side would call their opponents "curs." It was all in good fun, Mariam thought.

A boy and a girl, both about her sister's age or maybe a bit older, were chasing each other for possession of the fortress, screaming "cur" and "infidel" at each other as they ran. There was a woven carpet spread out under the shade of a tree where a woman sat with a girl younger than Onnig at her feet. She was keeping one eye on the older children playing while she shelled almonds into an earthen bowl. The little girl was making a pyramid of nut shells in the dirt beside the carpet.

Mariam, her sister and little brother in tow, walked over to where the woman sat. "My name is Mariam Hovsepian, and this is my sister, Marta, and our brother, Onnig."

The woman met Mariam's eyes and smiled. She was about the same age as Mariam's mother, and she had the same kindly work-worn look about her.

"Are you with the barley workers?" she asked.

"Yes," said Mariam. "We've travelled all the way from Marash."

"Sit down," said the woman, patting a space on the carpet beside her.

Mariam sat down, but Marta stayed standing. She was more interested in playing "Turks and Armenians" than talking to an old married woman.

Onnig looked uncertainly at the little girl on the carpet playing with the nut shells, but didn't make a move to sit down. The little girl looked up and smiled at Onnig. Then she noticed Marta's doll.

"Dolly," the girl said with excitement. She reached out to touch it.

Mariam noticed the frown that was beginning to form on Marta's brows. Before her little sister could say anything, Mariam asked, "Would you like to hold it?"

The girl grinned.

Mariam gave her sister a meaningful look. Marta sighed, then handed the doll over. "Just be careful with it," she said.

Then she ran over to play ball with the older children, Onnig in tow.

"My name is Anoush Adomian," said the woman, extending a callused hand to Mariam. "And this is my daughter, Arsho."

Arsho was so busy admiring the rag doll that she barely looked up when she heard her mother use her name. "And that is my son, Kevork," she said, pointing towards the boy playing ball. "The girl is our neighbour, Taline."

Mariam found it cool and pleasant to sit under the tree with Anoush. It was a welcome relief after so many days on the dusty road. Anoush was full of questions about life in Marash, and Mariam answered her while keeping one eye on Onnig. She listened to Anoush's comments with half an ear. She wasn't worried about Marta at all. Marta was certainly old enough to handle herself, but Onnig was much younger than the others. She was just waiting for a crisis. Any minute now, he would burst into tears and run to her arms for comfort, full of stories of how the big kids were picking on him.

It surprised her, then, when it didn't happen. Instead of ignoring the little boy and playing around him, Kevork and Taline made a point of including both Marta and Onnig in their game. They both seemed genuinely delighted to have other children to play with, even though one was so young.

"… so it surprised me to see you," continued Anoush.

"I'm sorry, what did you say?" Mariam asked.

"With the unrest," said Anoush. "It's not a good time for women and children to be away from home."

"My mother wanted us all to stick together right now," explained Mariam.

"I have heard rumour of massacres," said Anoush. "But I don't believe it. Who would get the grain in if the Armenians were killed?"

"Indeed," said Mariam.

After that first day, Mariam made a point of taking her younger siblings to the village whenever she could so that they could play with the other children. There were chores to do at the camp, like washing clothing, preparing food, and gathering kindling. Sometimes Kevork and Taline would walk up to the camp to find Onnig and Marta. Whenever they did this, Mariam was happy to let them all play while she did her chores, as long as they kept close enough for her to keep an eye on them. It was hardly necessary, though, because the children were so good with Onnig.

One morning in the middle of April, Mariam finished her chores, then gathered Onnig and Marta and headed down to the village.

As they approached the village gates, they didn't stop to notice the eerie silence. The little one-storey clay homes all seemed empty. Even the goats and chickens were quiet. The children walked down the street all the way to the well without meeting a soul. The dama table was abandoned, although it looked like a game had been in progress just moments before.

The open-air market stalls were unmanned, although there were some lemons, wicker baskets, cheese, and other goods that had been in the process of being laid out for display. Mariam looked over at the church and noticed that the doors, usually kept open, were closed tight. She walked up to the church door and put her ear to it. She could hear frightened whispers of people inside. She put her hand on the elaborately carved wooden handle and pulled, but it was locked, so she knocked on the door and called, "Is anybody in there?" The frightened whispers stopped. Mariam could almost hear a collective gasp of fear.

Suddenly, Mariam could feel vibrations rumbling at her feet and she heard a sound — something like thunder — in the distance. It was coming from the direction of the village gates, and when she looked that way she saw a cloud of dust and angry-looking men on horses. Some of them carried bayonets, and some carried torches.

Mariam ran to Onnig and picked him up in her arms, then she ran down the street. "Marta, follow me," she called.

Marta looked from Mariam to the rumbling of men, then ran after her sister.

There was only one way to go, and that was in the opposite direction of the village gates. They ran through the maze-like streets, past the house where Taline lived. Then past where Kevork and Arsho lived with Anoush, and past the bathhouse. They passed another common courtyard area, and soon they were in a part of the village they had never seen before.

Suddenly, a gunshot pierced the silence. Mariam instinctively placed a hand over Onnig's mouth.

A woman's scream.

Onnig struggled in his sister's arms, trying to cry out in protest, but her hand remained clamped over his mouth. "We have to hide," Mariam whispered to her sister.

There was a bush not too far away, so they ran to it and fell in a heap behind it.

"I dropped Bibi," whispered Marta, glancing tearfully out into the courtyard at her doll.

"Forget Bibi," hissed Mariam.

At that comment, Onnig bit Mariam's fingers and wailed. "I want my mommy!"

"Shut up," Mariam whispered frantically. But Onnig kept on wailing. Mariam was about to slap him hard across the face but stopped, her hand poised in mid-air. "You must be quiet, Onnig. They'll kill us if they find us." Onnig's eyes were suddenly round with fear, and he let out one loud sob, but then covered his own mouth with both hands. Mariam breathed a sigh of relief. She was glad that Onnig understood.

Once she got her bearings, Mariam realized that the bush they were hiding behind was in front of a mosque. They were in the Turkish district. Even on the best of days, Mariam would have been reluctant to be seen in the Turkish district, and this was certainly not the best of days. A shuffle of movement could be heard inside the mosque. Mariam realized that there were people hiding in the mosque just as there had been people hiding in the church at the other end of the village. She froze in fear. What if someone stepped out now and found them?

How can we get out of this mess? she thought in desperation. She took a deep breath to calm herself. She was the oldest, and her parents trusted her to look after Marta and Onnig. She looked up at the roof of the mosque and noticed that it was not much higher than the houses in the area. It wouldn't be that hard to get on top of it. Better yet, she noticed that this was a very old style of mosque that had recently been outfitted with a new flat roof of tin, unadorned by domes and minarets. With calmness she didn't feel, she turned to Marta and whispered, "If you climb onto my shoulders, can you hoist yourself up to the roof?"

Marta looked up uncertainly, then looked back at her sister in panic. "There are people inside. What if they hear us?"

"Do it quietly," replied Mariam unhelpfully. Then she squatted down and hiked up her sister like she'd done dozens of times when they were playing. Only this time the reward wasn't forbidden figs: if they were lucky, they might not be killed.

With difficulty, Marta silently scrambled onto the roof, scraping her hands and knees on the sharp metal edge of the corrugated rooftop in the process. Mariam looked up and saw her sister standing on the roof, mesmerized by something she saw in the Armenian district.

"Grab Onnig," Mariam hissed.

Marta squatted down. She draped a portion of her long skirt over the sharp metal edge to protect her baby brother. Mariam had Onnig balanced precariously on her shoulders, his eyes round with fear and his arms flailing in the air. Marta reached down and grabbed him under the arms. The sudden weight of her brother made her almost pitch forward.

"Boost him to me on the count of three," she called down to Mariam.

Mariam had her arms firmly gripped around her bother's waist. At the count of three, she lifted him as high as she could, his feet dangling in the air. Marta pulled him towards her and she fell backwards. He flew through the air and landed with a thump on her chest, knocking the wind out of her.

Onnig was shaking with fear, and a loud sob escaped from deep in his throat. The sound of the sob sent Marta into panic mode. What if the people in the mosque heard?

She held up a finger to her lips and said, "Shhh." Onnig gulped back another sob, then nodded to his sister. He lay still beside her on her spread-out skirt and clamped his hands across his mouth. She could only pray that the people inside didn't think too much about the noise.

Marta looked over the side of the roof to see how Mariam was doing. Mariam had managed to find a piece of wood and had propped it against the wall. Stepping onto the top of the wood, she gingerly scrambled onto the roof. She spread out her skirt on the hot metal, then flattened herself down on the other side of Onnig and closed her eyes. There the three children remained, baking in the sun, for what seemed like hours, listening to the sounds of screaming in the distance. To the sisters' relief, Onnig was silent.

The door of the mosque was pushed open. One man came out and walked to the middle of the road. He shielded his eyes with his hands, then peered out towards the Armenian district. "It is done," he said.

When the man walked back towards the mosque, Mariam cringed in fear, hoping that he wouldn't see them. Mercifully, he didn't look up.

He opened the door to the mosque and she heard clearly what he said to the people inside: "It is safe to go home now."

Mariam heard the rustling of silks and more footsteps as the mosque emptied. She caught snatches of conversation.

"This isn't right," a woman's voice said. "They should never have come right into the village for the killings."

"But how else to get to the infidels?" asked another voice. "After all, the Sultan gave permission for these killings. They were only doing their duty."

As Mariam listened to the bits of conversation, hearing words like "traitors" and "outsiders," she tried to piece together what was going on.

The children stayed still long after the last footsteps echoed in the distance. Finally, Mariam stretched out her cramped body and peered over the edge of the roof. "It's safe," she whispered. She stood up on the roof. "Follow me," she said to Marta. Then she picked up Onnig and placed him on her hip.

As they walked across the Turkish roofs, Mariam was startled to see that houses that had looked so plain from the street were actually quite opulent within their gates.

Marta caught up with her. "I want to walk in the street," she said, her eyes round with concern.

"It's safer up here," said Mariam.

Marta's eyes filled with tears. "But my dolly is in the street."

Mariam opened her mouth to argue, then thought better of it. Who was to know what they would be losing today? If she could minimize that pain for her sister by just a little bit, then why not?

"Okay," she said. "Let's get down." Onnig scrambled off her hip and stood beside Marta.

Mariam lowered herself over the side of the house, using a window as a ledge, then dropped down into a vegetable patch. As she reached up for Onnig, Mariam's eyes were directly in front of the window. Through the latticework, she was startled to see a woman's eyes staring out at her. Mariam stared boldly back, as if challenging the woman to do something, but the eyes disappeared. Mariam reached up and Marta carefully placed Onnig into her arms. Marta jumped clumsily down and landed with a thud in the garden. The garden gate was fastened with a large hook, so Mariam undid it, then she and her brother and sister walked out onto the street.

It was eerily silent.

As they walked down the middle of the street, more than one set of eyes stared out at them, but nobody stopped them.

Marta's doll was still in the street, exactly where she dropped it. She picked it up.

The children walked towards the burning Armenian quarters, Onnig compliant and trembling on Mariam's hip. The wooden gate on the courtyard of Anoush Adomian's house had been kicked in. There were no chickens and no goat in the garden.

Mariam looked over to Marta with a question in her eyes, and Marta nodded imperceptibly. Mariam let Onnig down off her hip, and he grasped Marta's hand. The two younger children waited in the courtyard while Mariam stepped into the central corridor of the house. "Anoush?" she called. No answer. "Kevork?" No answer.

She stepped into the main room. There were two ovens. One was the *tonir* — an oven dug into the middle of the earthen floor that was for warmth and family gathering, not for cooking. On top of the tonir was a flat, raised, table-like top covered with a large carpet. The Adomians' sleeping cushions were still in a circle around the tonir, and there was a half-eaten piece of flatbread and a handful of figs on the table-like top in the centre.

The other oven was the cooking hearth, or *ojak*, at the side of the room. Mariam saw that a knife had been dropped on the ground in front of it, and a big clay cooking pot full of stew had smashed to the ground. The juice of the stew had sunken into the dirt floor, leaving scraps of nut and vegetable scattered about. A carpet loom had taken up a large space in front of the fireplace, but now it was mangled, and the half-finished carpet had been sliced to shreds. Arsho's cradle had been cut from the rope that suspended it from the ceiling and it had fallen precariously close to the fire. Mariam stepped over to it and looked inside. Empty.

Bile rose in her throat as she imagined what must have happened to her friends. She walked back out the door.

When Mariam stepped out of the house, Marta looked at her with a question in her eyes, but Mariam just shook her head.

Next, they checked in Taline's house, but no one was there, either.

They walked further down the street to the common area in the Armenian district. The market stalls had been kicked in and burned, and the dama board was knocked over, game pieces scattered in the dirt.

The worst was the church. The elaborately carved doors had been bolted from the outside so that no one could escape. And then it had been set on fire.

Some people tried to save themselves by jumping out the windows, but the Turks had planned for that.

Mariam gripped Onnig to her tightly as she looked at the faces of the corpses around the church. Some she recognized. There was the lemon vendor, and one of the old men who played dama.

Mariam felt Onnig suddenly gasp. She looked at his eyes and followed his gaze. He was staring at his dead friend Taline, her head at an awkward angle with a boot mark on her face. Onnig covered his mouth with both hands and stifled his sobs. Mariam rubbed her brother's back, trying to calm and comfort him, but where was there comfort? Certainly not here.

Hugging her brother tight, Mariam walked away from the church and continued down the road and out through the village gates. She had to find out whether her parents were all right. She didn't turn to see if Marta was following. She knew that her sister was right by her side. She could hear her gasping back her sobs.

The fields were littered with threshing tools, but not a worker was in sight.

Mariam's eyes scanned the fields. She spotted her mother's sickle. On it was a single drop of blood. Mariam picked it up and wiped the blood off with her finger, then tucked it carefully into the back of her belt as she had seen her mother do.

"Maybe they had time to hide," she said hopefully, searching the area for possibilities.

"What about the caves?" asked Marta.

They walked, hearts pounding, toward the first cave. Marta held Onnig firmly on her hip while Mariam peered in, calling, "Mairig? Boba? Are you there?"

She looked at her siblings' anxious eyes. "I can't see anything," she said. "It's too dark."

The children went back to the camping area and found a candle and matches. Mariam didn't tell her brother and sister why she was doing it, but she also rooted through her mother's rucksack and withdrew a vial of oil and all three of her mother's packed veils. She put the container of oil in her pocket and tied all of the veils around her shoulders, on top of her own. They returned to the cave and again Mariam entered. The cave was empty.

In eerie silence, they searched cave after cave. Finally, they approached one that was far away from their camping area. This one looked large enough to hold many people. Marta held Onnig close, caressing the back of his neck to calm his trembling, while Mariam lit the candle, then entered.

The cave was huge and wide at the mouth, and then it narrowed into smaller pathways. As Mariam approached one of the smaller openings, she stepped into something slick and had to grip onto the side of the cave to keep her balance. She lowered the candle to her feet and saw that the slickness was just as she feared: blood.

She swallowed back fear and sadness and anger and bile. She was the oldest, and she had to find out if her parents were here. She stood up and extended the candle in front of her as far as it would reach. Suddenly, the opening was illuminated. Armenians hacked to death. All men. She made herself look carefully at the faces. Neither her uncle nor father was in the group.

Although they were dead, there was still one last thing she could do for them. She drizzled a bit of the oil from the vial onto the tip of the index finger on her right hand. She made a circle with her thumb and index finger, and made a sign of the cross in the air. She untied one of the veils and lightly draped it over the corpses. She bent down and scooped a small handful of pebbles from the ground and scattered them on the veil, and then she recited the traditional Armenian prayer for the dead.

Not a proper burial, but at least their souls would rest in peace.

With the candle to guide her, she looked for another opening. The next one she found had no blood at the entrance, but she shone her candle in just in case. A single migrant worker dead. One of the leering men from the barn.

Because there was only one, and she could step in closer, she dotted the man's brow and hands and feet with the oil in a sign of the cross, and then she ripped a strip from one of the veils and draped it over him — symbolic of a shroud. She finished the ritual, then backed away.

Her gruesome journey of discovery continued. Difficult as it was, she had to find her own parents. She knew it immediately when she finally found them. When she shone her candle into the opening, the first thing that set this group apart was her mother's dirt-encrusted wool skirt. She was curled into a tight ball and she looked like she was sleeping, except for the slit across her throat, and all the blood. Her father and uncle were crammed into the crevice in front of her, as if they had tried to protect her to the death.

Mariam reached in. She touched her mother's face. Then she reached to her father's face and closed his eyes, then she did the same with her uncle.

She could see the skin of water still fastened around her mother's waist, so Mariam reached in and unfastened it. With the water, she would be able to perform a more complete burial observance.

She ripped off a strip of cloth from the already ripped veil and saturated it with water. She dabbed her parents' and uncle's faces and hands and feet with the wet cloth in a ritual cleansing, and then anointed the brows and hands and feet with oil in the sign of the cross. She had her mother's last veil left, and so she lovingly draped it across the corpses.

Mariam had a feeling like being out of her own body and watching down as this strangely calm girl-woman went through the motions. She was beyond emotion, and in some ways she felt that she was beyond death. There was only one thing she could think of at the moment, and that was to give her family the traditional Armenian burial they would have wanted. A shiver went through her as she dropped pebbles onto the veil. For a moment she thought she heard her mother's voice saying, "Look after your brother and sister."

She said one last silent prayer, then left the cave.

Her eyes took awhile to adjust when she was finally out of the cave again, and the first thing she saw was the strained looks on the faces of her brother and sister. She nodded grimly to them. "They're dead," she said. "But they are in heaven now." Is there a heaven? she wondered. Wherever they were, it was better than this.

Onnig and Marta enveloped her in their arms. The children huddled together in their grief, and soon they fell into an exhausted sleep.

Mariam heard dogs howling in her sleep and woke up with a start. She looked around her and saw that it was still broad daylight and very hot. Onnig was soundlessly asleep, but Marta was whimpering. Mariam gently shook her sister's shoulder until she opened her eyes.

"We should cover the mouth of the cave," said Mariam. She didn't want to say out loud what her fears were — that wild dogs would tear apart the flesh of their dead family. The thought was too gruesome to share.

Marta looked at her older sister and nodded. "Yes," she said.

In a frenzy of energy, the sisters gathered stones and twigs and piled them up at the mouth of the cave. Marta fashioned a crucifix from two straight sticks, then leaned it against the front of the cave. Mariam placed a lit candle in front of it. Then they roused Onnig, and the three children prayed.

CHAPTER TWO

Mariam was jolted awake by a hand placed on her shoulder. She clutched Onnig, who was asleep in her lap, and squinted her eyes open. It was Kevork. He was with an odd-looking white-haired woman.

Mariam sat up. She was confused that Kevork was alive, and she was confused by this strange companion of his. "We were at your house but we couldn't find you ..."

"I know," said Kevork. "I saw you."

Onnig opened his eyes to the sound of the familiar voice. When he saw Kevork, he tumbled out of his sister's lap and ran to him. "Where have you been?" Onnig asked.

Kevork sat down on the ground and took Onnig in his arms. He nuzzled his nose into Onnig's downy hair and thought of Arsho. "It will be fine," said Kevork, rocking the child gently. "You're safe. Thank God."

Kevork felt comfort in the closeness of the child, but it also sharpened his sense of loss. His mind suddenly filled with the memory of Mariam when she had stepped into his house the day before. He had watched her from his hiding place in the rafters, his heart pounding with fear. When he first heard her footsteps, he thought the Turks had come back.

It had been more than the sound of footsteps that had sent him up to the rafters in the first place. His mother had just put stew on to simmer, and the knife that had chopped the vegetables was still resting on the cooking hearth. She was in the courtyard, gathering figs for breakfast.

Arsho was napping in her cradle, suspended by a rope from the rafters. One end of the rope had been tied to the loom so that as Anoush wove the intricate patterns into her prized carpets, Arsho would be rocked to sleep.

But the morning coziness had been shattered when his mother stepped back into the house, fear in her eyes, but with resolute calm. "Hide," she said urgently, pointing to the rafters.

Kevork stepped onto the table-like top of the tonir and hoisted himself up. From his hiding spot, he watched as his mother threw the handful of figs on the tonir, and, with shaking hands, took the knife from the hearth and hid it in the flap of her waistband. Then, with careful urgency so as not to wake the child, she pulled the rope to Arsho's cradle all the way up to the rafters and secured it with a knot. She was about to step onto the tonir to hoist herself up into the rafters beside her son when the door burst open. Kevork willed himself not to cry out in fear as he watched his mother quickly drop down onto his cushion and pretend that she was calmly eating her breakfast.

A soldier holding a bayonet, smelling of smoke, stepped in. "Where's your man?" he asked Anoush.

"Dead," she replied.

Kevork listened to his mother's lie. His father was away, selling carpets, but the answer seemed simpler.

"You're alone?" he asked, inspecting the dim interior with a quick glance.

"Yes," she said.

Kevork held his breath.

Arsho whimpered.

The soldier looked into the rafters and spied the cradle. Kevork willed himself to be invisible. "Typical lying Armenian bitch," said the soldier, then spat on the floor. "What else are you hiding? Where are your weapons?"

He walked over to where the cradle was suspended, then severed its rope with a single slash of the bayonet. The cradle crashed to the floor. Arsho wailed. The soldier raised his bayonet as if to strike the baby.

In a flash, Anoush had the kitchen knife to the soldier's throat. "Leave my daughter alone," she growled.

From above, Kevork shook in fear. What was his mother thinking? The soldier was twice her size. He had to save his mother. Without making a sound, he positioned himself to jump down on the soldier, but there was a loud crashing sound. The soldier and his mother struggled, knocking over the loom. Then his mother kicked hard at the pot, sending scalding stew splattering over the soldier, who cried in pain, but also over little Arsho, whose wailing became even louder.

"That's enough," said the soldier. Then he gripped Anoush's wrist so tightly that the knife clattered to the ground.

Kevork watched in horror as the soldier kicked the cradle hard, knocking Arsho onto the floor. The child stopped crying. Then the soldier picked up his mother, as if she were nothing more than a sack of cloth, and walked out the door.

Kevork was utterly confused by what he had witnessed. The soldier had not killed his mother. He had taken her. Kevork had heard stories of things like this, but in the stories, the woman always killed herself to save her soul. A jumble of emotions rushed through Kevork's mind. The Turk had knocked the knife out of his mother's hand so she couldn't kill him — or herself. What was happening to her now? Kevork tried not to think about it. The important thing was that she might still be living. But if she was living, did that mean she had lost her soul?

Kevork was immobilized with fear and confusion and horror. It was his sister's continued silence that made him finally lower himself down from the rafters and step onto the tonir. He walked over to where his sister lay amidst the bits of stew and upended cradle. She looked like she was sound asleep. A wave of relief washed over Kevork. It was only when he bent to gather her in his arms that he realized she was limp in death.

He sat cradling his sister's body for uncounted moments, and it was then that he heard footsteps and voices. Fearing that the Turks had returned, he placed Arsho's body in the rafters, then hoisted himself up beside her. He watched below as Mariam, not a Turk, entered his house. He was relieved to see that she was alive, but he was too full of sorrow to speak.

Later, Kevork ventured out to find his friends. Now he sat in front of the cave rocking Onnig on his lap, enveloped in his memories.

Mariam looked over and saw that Marta was sitting up, rubbing sleep out of her eyes. Then Mariam looked up at the woman who had accompanied Kevork. She wasn't very old: perhaps twenty. But she had abnormally pale skin and stark white hair hanging loose down her back. Her eyes looked pink-rimmed and sore, and the irises were a frightening blue instead of the usual dark brown. Mariam tried not to stare. She had seen women with yellow hair before, and many older women had white hair, of course, but she had never seen anyone who had the colouring of this woman. Mariam felt an involuntary shudder run up her spine.

Kevork lifted his face from Onnig's hair and noticed Mariam's gaze. "This is my aunt Anna Adomian," he said.

The woman looked Mariam in the eyes and bowed slightly. Mariam felt ashamed of herself. She imagined that this woman got stared at a lot for her appearance.

Mariam stood up and brushed the dirt from her dress, then she extended her hand to Anna. "Glad to meet you," she said. Then she introduced her brother and sister.

"I'm albino," said Anna.

"What?" asked Mariam, confused.

"I was born this way. My parents were dark like you."

"Oh," said Mariam, not really understanding.

"You must be thirsty," said Anna. She reached into the folds of her dress and drew out a skin of water. She opened it, then offered it to Onnig first.

"Yes please," he said, and opened his mouth expectantly. Anna squirted some water in, then offered the skin to Mariam.

The action reminded Mariam of her mother, and she had to will herself not to cry.

Anna looked beyond Mariam to the grave behind her. "Where shall you go now?" she asked.

"We have no place here," said Mariam. "We must get back to Marash."

"You cannot go to Marash right now," said Anna. "Come to the village with us."

"But the village is destroyed."

"Not completely," said Anna.

"I won't go," said Onnig, scrambling from Kevork's lap and walking towards the rock-covered entrance of the cave.

"Onnig, my soul," said Mariam.

"Mommy and Daddy will come back. I know."

"They're dead," Mariam said softly.

Onnig shook his head stubbornly.

"Mommy and Daddy are in heaven."

"No," said Onnig.

He banged at the rocks. "Mommy, Daddy, wake up."

Kevork walked over to Onnig and picked him up, dodging his thrashing arms and legs. "Let them sleep for now," he said. "We'll come back for them later. Let's go," he called over his shoulder to the others as he walked briskly, carrying the kicking, crying boy with him.

Mariam glanced longingly back at the mouth of the cave as she followed the rest of the group. Her heart was filled with heavy sadness. So many times she had chafed under the watchful eyes of her mother and father. And so many times she had complained about her poor lot in life. What she would give now to turn time back a few pages and have her parents alive and their family whole again.

Recent footsteps had made a pathway from the cave to the fields, and she followed the others as they walked down it. Onnig was still wailing in Kevork's arms, but he was no longer struggling. It was quick thinking on Kevork's part, she thought, to take charge with Onnig. Not that it made a whole lot of difference in the long run. Would the devastated village be any safer for them than the cave of graves?

"Allah is great. Some of you live."

The voice startled Mariam from her thoughts. It was the boss. The Turk who had given their family a job and a place to stay.

He stood before the weary group on the path in the middle of his barley field. He was pushing a wheelbarrow. Mariam could see that it was filled with sickles and other farming implements. He had been collecting the tools that had been left scattered in his fields when the attacks occurred. Mariam could feel a new wave of sadness rise in her throat: each sickle represented one Armenian, and here they were, piled up like so much garbage.

Mariam's first reaction was a feeling of hatred for this man. He was a Turk, and it was Turks who had killed her family. But he looked kind and distraught, and not at all threatening.

"You are the only ones I have found alive," he said. "My name is Abdul Hassan. Come back to the migrant camp where you will be safe."

As Anna stepped forward to speak to the man, Mariam noticed that a wave of fear crossed his face and he gripped the blue ceramic bead that hung from a strap around his neck — his amulet to ward off the Evil Eye.

Anna was of course familiar with the effect her appearance had on people, so she lowered her eyes and said, "Thank you for your kind offer, sir, but we must get back to the village."

"As you wish," said Abdul Hassan. "But at least let me feed you."

He manoeuvred the wheelbarrow to turn down the pathway. They followed, Onnig whimpering quietly, still in Kevork's arms.

The Turk's house was a few hundred yards beyond the barn where the male migrant workers had stayed. It was two storeys tall and made of mud bricks like those in the village. It was bigger than the homes in the Armenian district, but not as large as many in the Turkish district. Instead of a bricked-in courtyard, the garden could be seen from a distance. A goat and a few chickens ran free.

A stout woman with her hair completely covered under a long veil and a gauzy yashmak over the bottom of her face stepped out of the cottage and shielded her eyes with one hand so she could get a better look at her husband and his guests. She surmised the situation quickly, and disappeared back through the doorway. Moments later she came out carrying a rolled up carpet.

"This is my wife, Amina Hanim," he said to Anna and the children. Amina bowed deeply.

Her husband took the carpet from her, and she went back inside. He spread the carpet on the ground. "Please sit down," he said. "I will be right back."

Mariam looked at Anna with a question in her eyes, and Anna nodded imperceptibly. "Very well," said Mariam. "I guess we'll sit."

Mariam sat down, then reached up to Kevork, who was still holding onto Onnig. Kevork loosened the little boy's grip around his neck and placed him in his sister's lap. Onnig had stopped whimpering and was looking around in curiosity.

Marta settled in beside her sister, then Anna and Kevork found spots on the carpet too.

Mariam looked at the strange group. Here they all were, sitting on a carpet waiting for food. They had been orphaned by Turks, yet here they were, being fed by Turks. It was all so odd.

Amina Hanim came out with a tray holding a large earthen pitcher and several tall clay glasses. She knelt down and placed the tray in the middle of the carpet, lifted up the pitcher and poured a creamy thick beverage into each of the glasses, then gave one to each of her guests.

Mariam sniffed the contents of her glass, then sipped. It was a delicious yogurt drink the Turks called *ayran* and Armenians called *tan*.

Abdul Hassan came out of the house, bearing a platter of food. He set it on the carpet beside the tray of tan. There was a stack of Turkish tonir bread cut in wedges, black olives, cheese, and sliced wild cucumbers. Mariam reached forward and took a wedge of the Turkish bread. She ripped off a large chunk and put it in her mouth. It amazed her how good it tasted. Amidst all the terror and sadness of the last twenty-four hours, Mariam hadn't once considered food, but now she was famished. The bread was aromatic with a hint of yogurt and yeast and salt, and it was quite different from the unleavened Armenian flatbread. She tore off another chunk and gave it to Onnig. He ate it hungrily.

The husband and wife sat silently at the edge of the carpet, watching their guests eat. Each time someone finished their glass of yogurt, the woman would pour out some more, and she went back into the house when the platter was nearly empty and came back with a bowl of nuts and figs.

In normal times, Onnig would have eaten quickly and then gotten up to play. These were not normal times, however, so he sat quietly on his sister's lap long after he had eaten his fill.

"The killing is finished," said Abdul Hassan, as his wife gathered up the remnants of the picnic. "The Sultan's amnesty period is over."

Mariam frowned in confusion. "What do you mean, amnesty period?" she asked.

"Sultan Abdul Hamid proclaimed a twenty-four-hour grace period for crimes against infidels," explained the Turk. "The grace period is up. Turks who kill now risk being prosecuted."

"That is good to know," said Mariam, although she didn't feel good about it at all. Her parents and who knows how many others had just been killed in a state-sanctioned action.

"The village has been decimated," said Abdul Hassan. "And although the immediate risk is over, I don't know how safe it is for Armenians. You are welcome to stay in the barn. I could probably find some work for you to do."

Kevork looked up from his place on the carpet. "My house in the village is still standing," he said. "We'll go there."

As the Turk regarded the motley assortment of survivors, Mariam could see the sympathy in his eyes. "The little boy," said Abdul Hassan. "It will be difficult for him in the village. Amina Hanim and I have no children. We could adopt him."

Mariam hugged Onnig tightly to her and willed herself not to sob out loud. She knew Abdul Hassan was being kind, but she couldn't bear the thought of her brother being raised by someone else. "Thank you for your offer," she said. One hot tear rolled down her cheek. "But we would like to stay together."

"You could stay together in the barn," said the man, not unkindly.

The offer was all wrong, and Mariam knew it. If they stayed at all, Onnig would grow up thinking he was Turkish. And to stay in the barn and work for this man was not a possibility. The barn just recently housed the migrant workers who had been massacred, and their own parents had been massacred right on this land. Mariam couldn't imagine the nightmares she would have here.

"Or we could take you and your sister and the little boy into our house," he offered.

Even though she would still be with her brother and sister, and even though they would be fed and clothed, and perhaps even loved, she did not want to grow up as a Turk. Onnig was clinging to her and trembling slightly in her arms. He seemed to have an inkling of what the Turk was offering. And she could tell by his reaction that this wasn't something he wanted, either. She looked at her sister. Marta caught her eye and shook her head slightly. Mariam looked at Anna and Kevork. They remained silent, but their eyes were sorrowful. What would happen to them? wondered Mariam. A deformed woman and a young boy alone had no chance of survival.

Mariam looked at the Turk and shook her head. "Thank you," she said, "but I think we will all stick together."

"At least let me give you something," said the Turk. "Your parents had not been paid yet for all their work. I will give you that."

Mariam nodded. Her parents had earned that money. With blood.

The man rose to his feet, then stretched out his hand to help up Anna, then Mariam and Marta. "Your family's supplies are here too," he said.

He went into his house and came back with a small purse of gold. "Here," he said, thrusting it into Mariam's hands. She tucked it into her belt beside her mother's sickle.

They followed Abdul Hassan down to the place that had been their encampment. Mariam held back a sob as she looked at their humble pot for pilaf and their sleeping carpets. Her whole world had shifted, yet nothing had changed.

"Those are yours," said the Turk, gesturing towards the meagre supplies. "And take what you need from the barn."

Mariam knew that if she tried to say anything out loud, she would burst into tears, so instead she simply nodded at Abdul Hassan. This constant mention of the barn upset her greatly. The last thing she wanted to do was to go into the migrants' barn and root around the dead men's belongings for something good. Leave that for some other scavenger.

She slung her father's rucksack onto her back and helped Marta shrug into their uncle's. Kevork and Anna gathered up what they could, and then the little group thanked the Turk for his kindness and headed back down to the village.

Walking through the village gates was an eerie experience. Instead of the faint scent of lemon and the happy shrieks of children, there was a sharp smell of ashes and cold silence.

Survivors had collected their dead off the streets, and Mariam could only imagine the many burial rituals that were happening in silence in the houses that surrounded her. She was overcome by sadness. They walked all the way to Kevork's house without encountering a single soul.

When she stepped through the gate of the court-yard, the first thing she noticed was freshly turned soil under the mulberry tree. She didn't ask: she knew this was Arsho's grave.

Inside, the house was much like she had seen it last. Mice had come and cleaned up the remnants of the stew from the floor and the figs from the now-cold ojak. She was grateful to see that Kevork had put away the cradle. Onnig was unsettled enough already, and the sight of the broken cradle would have grieved him beyond despair, she was sure.

Mariam set down the rucksack, then went to the ojak and stirred the ashes, looking for cinders. There were none. She opened up her father's rucksack and drew out a package of prized matches. Taking some kindling from a stack at the side of the ojak, she lit a small fire. The ojak was the heart of any Armenian home. And she had to put heart back into this one.

CHAPTER THREE

For Kevork, that first evening was the hardest. The day of the massacres, he had been in shock, but now the shock was subsiding and the sadness was sinking in.

While Mariam lit the ojak, Kevork mournfully dismantled his mother's broken loom. The wood was no better than firewood, it had been crushed so badly. He lovingly unhooked the half-made carpet and folded it carefully so that it wouldn't fray where it had been slashed by the soldier's bayonet. He found his mother's favourite veil — a solid swath of sky blue — and used that to wrap up the carpet. It was his last remnant of his mother.

When it was time for them to sleep that night, Kevork took down the three sleeping pillows: one for Anna, one for Marta, one for Mariam. Then he rooted around in the rafters and found a small pillow that his mother had woven and put away for safekeeping. It was supposed to have been for Arsho when she was old enough to sleep out of her cradle. He gave that one to Onnig. For himself, he used his mother's half-made carpet wrapped in her veil.

The night air was warm enough for sleeping outside, and for weeks, Kevork and his mother had carried Arsho's cradle to the roof and they had all slept in coolness under the stars with the faint scent of mulberry blossoms in the air. Sleeping outside this night was out of the question, however. There was a chill in the air that had nothing to do with the weather.

They arranged their pillows in a circle around the cold tonir instead. As he fell asleep that night, he buried his face in the veil. It still held the scent of his mother, so he breathed it in deeply and tried to suppress his sobs.

His eyes were still closed the next morning when he noticed the aroma of freshly brewed coffee. For a moment he thought that it had all been a very bad dream, but when he opened his eyes, he saw that it was Mariam sipping coffee at the fireplace, not his mother. A steaming demitasse sat in its saucer beside her on the hearth. She was going through the contents of her father's rucksack, a frown on her face.

She looked up. "We don't have much food left," she said.

"We have a sack of flour," said Kevork. "Also, raisins, olives, nuts, and oil."

"Anna found a ripped sack with flour spilled all over behind the house," said Mariam. "There is nothing else."

"There are still figs on the tree in the courtyard," said Kevork.

"Yes, there are," replied Mariam. "But your chickens are gone, and your goat. We're going to have to go to the market."

So once everyone was up and had eaten a light breakfast, they headed to the Armenian market.

But of course it was gone. Who was left to run it, after all? The houses in the Armenian district that weren't burnt down were either empty or barricaded tight.

"We still need food," said Anna.

Mariam had drawn out a few gold coins from the purse Abdul Hassan had given her, and these she held tightly in her hand. The purse itself was hidden under her belt. "Maybe we can go to the market in the Turkish district?"

In all the years that Kevork had lived in the village, he had never once been to the Turkish market. The two districts were so separate that there could have been a wall between them.

"I guess we have no choice," said Anna. "But first we must go home to prepare ourselves."

Anna wrapped her hair into a tight bun at the nape of her neck, then found one of Anoush's veils and secured it over her head, covering her hair entirely. Her eyes were really her most startling feature, and when she secured a yashmak over the bottom half of her face, her eyes were even more noticeable, but there was nothing she could do about that. She took Kevork by the hand and led the way.

Mariam followed, carrying Onnig on her hip, and Marta was at her side, her doll clutched protectively.

As they walked down the main street of the Turkish district, Kevork was painfully aware of the sensation they were causing. Children playing on the street were called in by their mothers, and doors were quickly closed. The men they passed were angry at the sight of Armenians in their district. Anna kept her eyes down, and so her unusual appearance was not immediately noticed.

Beyond the mosque was a canopied bazaar between two narrow streets. Anna slowed down and slipped behind the children and kept her gaze to the ground, well aware of the disturbance her appearance would create at closer scrutiny.

Mariam noticed that the vendor at one of the stalls seemed less hostile to their presence. While others looked the other way or pretended they were closed, this man regarded them with curiosity. The goods he sold were not as varied as some, but there were sacks of rice, onions, cucumbers, and raisins: items they sorely needed. She opened her palm and showed the man her coins. "Kind sir," she said timidly, "would you sell to us?"

At the sight of the coins, the man smiled. "What would you like?" he asked.

While Mariam bargained with the vendor, Kevork stood back and sized up the rest of the stalls. His eyes were drawn immediately to a familiar sight. At one of the stalls was tied his own goat, Sevo. Could it possibly be? He walked over to get a better look, and sure enough, this goat was solid black, except for a small brown splotch on her left side.

"Sevo!" he said with delight. He got down onto his knees and wrapped his arms around her. As he breathed in her familiar musky scent, tears sprung to his eyes. In finding Sevo he had salvaged a tiny bit of his beloved past. Sevo bleated in recognition and nuzzled her nose to Kevork's cheek.

The vendor stepped proprietarily beside the goat. "This is Ghara," he said. "I've had her for two years. Birthed her myself."

Kevork looked at the man skeptically. He knew the man was lying, but what did it matter? What police officer would believe an Armenian boy over a Turkish man?

Kevork waited for Mariam to finish her purchases, then motioned her and Anna over.

"How much is she?" asked Mariam. She recognized Sevo immediately. Anna stood a few steps back, her hair still covered and her eyes averted.

The man smiled. "Six lira."

"That is too much," said Kevork, with an angry flash in his eyes. "You stole this goat from my family, and now you are trying to steal her again."

"Then don't buy Ghara," the man said.

Anna stepped beside Mariam and Kevork, then raised her eyes. There was a sharp intake of breath from the vendor. He clutched the blue stone suspended on a strap around his neck and held up one hand, palm out. "It's the Evil Eye," he said. "Stay away."

"We want that goat," said Anna, gazing at him intently.

"Take it."

"We would also like two chickens," said Anna, relishing in the man's discomfiture.

"Four lira," the man said hastily. "My best two chickens and my beloved goat."

Mariam counted out the money and handed it to the vendor.

The man grabbed the coins, then shut up his booth.

Kevork grinned broadly as he led Sevo down the street by her rope. Over one shoulder was a sack of rice. Onnig carried one of the chickens, while Marta carried the other. When they were out of earshot, Kevork looked at his aunt. "Thanks," he said.

Anna smiled.

Chapter Four

As they stepped inside the steamy stone entranceway of the bathhouse and waited for the attendant to appear, Mariam looked around her nervously. "Are you sure we will be accepted?" she asked Kevork.

This was the first time they had attempted to go to the public bath since the massacre. It was located just outside the Turkish part of the village, in a neutral area, and was the one place where Armenians and Turks would mingle freely on a regular basis.

"This is the only public bath," replied Kevork. "Where else could we go?"

Mariam was dressed in a loose tunic and trousers, and she held Anoush's towel tightly to her chest, as if for protection. Marta was dressed similarly, and she also had an Adomian towel, as did Kevork, but they would have to rent ones for Onnig and Anna. She didn't need a full lira for the baths and towel rentals, so she had brought a handful of *piasters* — penny coins.

Just then, the bath attendant stepped through the entranceway. She was a hugely obese woman with a bun of greying hair hennaed red. The two large towels she was wrapped in gave her a semblance of modesty, but her massive arms were bare, and so were her calves. On her feet were *pattens* — a type of sandal on platforms used in bathhouses to keep the feet away from dirty, sudsy water. Her pudgy fingertips were pink and wrinkled from the vigorous scrubbings she'd been giving her clients all day.

"Good morning, Sophie Hanum," said Kevork, bowing his head slightly.

"Good morning, dear," she said, smiling at Kevork, then regarding the other people in his group.

"Why are you coming on women's day?"

Kevork usually came to the bathhouse with his father on Thursdays, but some nine-year-old boys still came on Tuesdays with their mothers. It was a borderline age to be let into the women's baths. "My father is away right now," said Kevork with a tremble in his voice. What Armenian in the village wasn't coming to the bathhouse with a changed family circumstance?

Sophie Hanum frowned and thought a moment. "There is no doubt you need a bath," she said, wrinkling her nose. She looked at the rest of the people in the group, and her eyes rested on Onnig. "Very well," she said. "You can go in. You'll be good company for the little one."

Kevork sighed with relief. He didn't want to go all alone on men's bath day. Mariam handed Sophie the fee for the baths and the extra towels and they walked in.

They were each led to separate rooms where they removed all of their clothing, then they were sudsed and soaped and shampooed and rinsed by bath attendants until their skin was pink and their hair shone clean. They met back up in the common area, where there was a huge pool of steamy water.

The bathhouse was a sociable place, and people gathered there for gossip as much as for cleanliness. Many people walked around completely naked, while others were loosely covered with silk wrap-arounds. It was bad form to be too bundled up in a bathhouse because it made others ill at ease. Without their clothes on, the children looked no different than the Turks. Even though everyone knew who they were, they were accepted without hostility. Even Anna was treated with courteous disregard.

Young children screamed and splashed, while their mothers and grandmothers looked on fondly. Onnig grinned for the first time in days and pulled Marta and Kevork into the warm water with him.

Stepping into the warm water brought back so many happy memories for Kevork, but it also reminded him of everything he had lost. When Kevork still came to the baths with his mother, he would meet up with Taline and his other friends. Sometimes, Taline would bring an air-filled sheep's bladder with her, and they would float on it together to the middle of the pool. But when he looked through the steamy dampness now, he didn't recognize a single playmate. It also felt very odd coming to this place without either his mother or his father. As the water swirled around him, Kevork felt like he was washing away his past.

Mariam's reaction was quite different from Kevork's. She was used to going to the baths in Marash with family members and she missed them dearly, but this unfamiliar bath did not evoke memories.

It confused her to watch the reaction on the women's faces when she walked in naked to the pool area. She knew the Turkish custom of women sizing up other women in the baths for the men in their families, but she didn't consider herself a woman yet. It also surprised her that they were sizing her up so intently, when she was just an Armenian.

Turkish men never got a chance to see what prospective brides looked like under the veil, and many stories circulated about rich men being tricked into marrying the ugly sister. The fact that women bathed together naked gave them a certain power over their men. First wives would try to ensure that their husband did not take on a second wife who was threateningly beautiful, and mothers tried to ensure the opposite.

Mariam blushed with embarrassment at the envious whispers and glances she was receiving. Mariam turned and looked at Anna. She was shocked to see bitterness on the woman's face, a mixture of anxiety and disapproval. That upset Mariam. After all, what had she done?

CHAPTER FIVE

As the weeks wore on, the survivors fell into a comforting routine. Anna, the only adult, was the nominal head of the household, but her ability to help the children was limited. While the Turks left her unmolested, they also left her unhired. There was no opportunity for her to earn money and look after the children she had become responsible for. All they had to live on was Mariam's purse of coins. With each succeeding week, the purse got lighter, and there was no means of refilling it.

Most of the surviving Armenians gradually moved out of the village and Turkish families took over the Armenian section. There were no children for Onnig, Marta, and Kevork to play with. So their house became a refuge and a prison. Each night, Mariam counted her piasters and liras, and each night she tried to estimate how much longer their money would last.

Once, when they were in the bathhouse, Mariam overheard a conversation between two Turkish women:

"The Sultan has been deposed." The woman who said this was young and pregnant, and she was sitting at the edge of the warm water pool with her feet dangling over the side. She had a towel loosely thrown over her shoulders, but otherwise, she was naked. She looked down at her friend, who was neck deep in the pool.

"He has?" exclaimed her companion in surprise. "By whom?"

"The Young Turks," replied the pregnant woman. "They're going to be putting the Sultan on trial."

Mariam's heart soared at this tidbit of information. Her parents had been supporters of the Young Turks when they briefly came to power in 1908. The Sultan's counter-revolution had been a shock to all. The Young Turk government had been promising freedom and democracy — even to non-Muslims. For the first time in weeks, Mariam felt like grinning.

As fall approached, there was a chill in the air, so Mariam lit the tonir before covering it with the sleeping carpet. Once they were all snuggled up under the carpet and ready for the usual evening of storytelling, Mariam announced, "It is time for us to leave the village."

Kevork had just settled into the warm carpet, but the announcement brought him up short. "Where would we go?"

"Home," said Mariam. "We have family in Marash."

Kevork didn't want to say it out loud, but he wondered whether her grandmother and aunt were still alive. Didn't the massacres happen there, too?

Mariam saw the look of pain on his face. "There is no way of knowing without going there," she said. Mariam knew what Kevork's real concern was: if they left, how would his parents find him? But they had waited long enough. "Besides," she continued, "with the Sultan deposed, it has to be safer for Armenians."

"We have money, a roof over our heads, and a supply of eggs and goat's milk," said Kevork. "It could be worse."

"We must get back to our family," said Mariam. "And once winter approaches, we'll have trouble travelling."

Kevork brushed his hand softly against the blue veil cover of his pillow. "I can't leave."

Mariam was silent. If there were a chance that her parents were alive, she'd be acting the same way.

Anna propped herself up on one elbow and looked at her nephew. "If your mother is alive," she said, "she is no longer the mother you knew. Put her out of your mind."

Kevork's face blushed bright red. "Don't say things about my mother. She was taken. She couldn't help it."

"The fact is," replied Anna, "that she ran off with a Turk." Anna had never been particularly fond of her beautiful sister-in-law.

Kevork swallowed back tears. The last thing he wanted was for his aunt to see how sorrowful he was at her statement. Armenian women who were taken by Turks had a moral duty to kill themselves. And she'd had a knife in her hand …

The scene flashed in his head again: the Turk had knocked the knife away. His mother couldn't kill herself. Was she alive? Did she wish she were dead? Honour or no, Kevork was glad there was still a chance that his mother was alive.

Mariam looked from Kevork to Anna. This was an ongoing discussion between the two. "It is not up to you to judge," she said to Anna. "You have never been in that situation."

Anna flinched.

"If either your mother or father is alive," continued Mariam, "they'll come here. You can leave them a note."

"How?" asked Kevork. "As soon as we leave, this house will be taken over by Turks."

"We can only hope that the new owners will pass on your message." Not a perfect solution, but what was?

The next few days were spent preparing food and packing.

Anna slaughtered the chickens, and they ate well for those last few days. Sevo would travel with them.

For Kevork, leaving the village was like closing a door on unfinished business. With sadness in his heart, he removed his mother's veil from the piece of carpet he had been using as a pillow and rolled it into a blue rope. He tied it around his waist like a belt. Then he went up into the rafters and searched through the items his mother had stored there. He found a pure white kite in the shape of a bird that his father had made him. How many days had he stood on the roof with his father as they threw the kite into the air and watched as it caught in the wind? He would have loved to take the kite with him, but he knew it wasn't practical, so he ran his finger against the wooden frame in a tribute of farewell, then set it aside.

He found a wool vest that his father would wear during the cold winter months when he travelled, selling Anoush's carpets. Kevork tried it on. It was way too long, reaching down to his knees, but he kept it on anyway, for memory as much as warmth. There was also a stack of swaddling cloth that had been used both for Kevork, when he was a baby, and for Arsho. He took a single length of it and held it to his face, breathing deeply. Who would look after Arsho's grave? He folded the cloth and tucked it into his blue belt.

Mariam's prized possession was her mother's small sickle. She sharpened it before the journey, then wrapped it in a cloth and stuck it in her belt. Marta had her doll, Bibi, and Onnig had become so attached to Arsho's small pillow that they decided to take it with them.

Mariam watched Anna go through the house one last time, but she realized that there was nothing of sentimental value for Anna to take with her. What must have her life been like before? wondered Mariam. She and her siblings had lost their parents, and Kevork had lost everything.

What was it that Anna had lost? She watched the woman coldly turn her back on the house, and then watched as her eyes lit up when Kevork and Marta and Onnig appeared. It seemed to Mariam that while the others had lost their loved ones, Anna had gained the only family she had ever known.

Anna and Mariam each wore rucksacks, and Kevork carried Onnig on his back. Marta, her doll on one hip, was in charge of Sevo, whom she led on a rope. Even Sevo had a job. Strapped across her back were several skins of water and Onnig's pillow.

As the little group walked down the main street and out through the village gates one last time, Mariam was struck with how much had changed in her life, yet how the world around them didn't seem to care. An outsider who walked through this village now wouldn't see anything amiss. What was once a thriving Armenian district was thriving once more. Gathered around the well were women with yashmaks covering their faces, gossiping while their husbands played dama under a tree. A barefooted boy darted past, nearly colliding into Mariam, as he chased one of his friends as they played "Turks and Armenians." It looked just the same as in April, except these people were all Turkish.

As they walked past what used to be the church, Mariam put her hand to her chest and gasped. She smelled the sharp scent of charring meat and her mind was filled with the grotesque images of the burning church. She realized with a start that her nose wasn't fooling her.

In the midst of the rubble of the church, a man had set up a barbecue and was selling freshly grilled lamb on a stick. He smirked when he saw the Armenians pass.

"Let's go quickly," said Mariam. The sooner they were out of this place, the better.

They went up to the cave grave one last time to pay their respects.

"I won't go," said Onnig stubbornly. He threw his wildflower bouquet down on the ground, then walked over to where Sevo was standing and put his arms around her neck.

"You don't have to," said Mariam. "Stay here with Kevork and Anna. We'll be back in a minute." She picked up the wildflower bouquet from the ground, then kissed her brother on the forehead. "I'll put this on their grave for you."

Mariam pulled a veil over her hair and smoothed down her dress with her free hand. Kevork and Anna and Onnig with Sevo stood at the end of the pathway leading to the cave that doubled as a grave. It would be easier for her and Marta to visit the grave this one last time without their brother anyway, Mariam rationalized.

The girls knelt side by side on the cold ground in front of the cave. Mariam could only hope that their parents' souls were now at peace. She felt a surge of grief fill her throat as she placed her bouquet and then her brother's down on the cold stone. She willed herself not to cry, but she noticed through the corner of her eye that her sister's bouquet glistened with a single hot tear.

From the pathway, Kevork watched the sisters at the grave. In one way, he envied them. At least they knew where their parents were. If his mother was still alive, how would she ever find him now? And what about his father? Was he really dead, or had he just taken off? At least Marta and Onnig and Mariam knew that they had been loved and that they hadn't been abandoned. Kevork felt so utterly alone. He also felt, that by leaving the village, he was abandoning any hope of ever finding his parents. He looked down at Sevo, whose mournful eyes looked back up at him, as if she understood his worries. He scratched her fondly between the ears and was thankful that at least he had her. Then he looked at the little boy whose arms were wrapped so tightly around the goat's neck, and he realized how much more he could have lost. Kevork at least had his memories. Would Onnig have that?

Kevork reached down and gathered Onnig into his arms, hugging him tight.

Mariam finished her prayer, then stood up, brushing the dust from her skirt. She reached down and tapped Marta on the shoulder, letting her sister know that it was time for them to leave.

They walked back down the path and found Onnig fast asleep in Kevork's lap, his arms thrown loosely around the older boy's neck. Kevork's head rested on Anna's shoulder and Anna held Sevo's rope with one hand. The goat grazed contentedly. More time had passed than they had realized.

They stretched, gathered together, and started their journey in earnest. As they walked down the grassy path towards the dirt road, Abdul Hassan came into view, and behind him was his wife, who was noticeably thinner than she had been the last time they saw her. Abdul Hassan had a sack of threshed fall wheat on his back and a sickle in one hand, and he looked exhausted. Amina Hanim's face, which was not covered with a yashmak, was red from the sun, and the edge of her veil was rimmed with sweat. She too held a sickle and a sack of wheat.

Abdul Hassan glanced at the rucksacks on their backs. "So you're leaving?" he asked.

Mariam stepped forward in greeting. "The time has come for us to find our way back to Marash."

The Turk's brow frowned with worry. "You cannot walk all the way back."

"We walked most of the way here," said Mariam.

"You were with a large group then," replied Abdul Hassan. "Now you are just children and one vulnerable woman."

"What shall we do?" asked Mariam.

The man was silent for a moment, deep in thought.

In the silence, words that Anoush had said to Mariam ages ago came back to her: *If they kill the Armenians, who will harvest the grain?*

Indeed. The Turk and his wife were alone in the field, threshing. The wheat was already going to seed. Mariam knew that if Abdul Hassan didn't get his crop in, he would face ruin.

Mariam caught Anna's eye and saw that she was thinking the same thing: perhaps if they helped Abdul Hassan with his harvest, he would help them get to Marash. "Perhaps we can help you?" Mariam asked.

The Turk looked at her hopefully, but not really understanding.

"We're children and one woman, that's true," said Mariam. "But we're strong. We could help bring in your wheat."

The Turk's eyes filled with gratitude. "Even one extra set of hands would be a blessing from Allah," he said. "We're about to lose the whole crop."

Amina Hanim took Mariam by the hand. "First we eat, then we work," she said, with a weary smile. Then she led the group up towards the house.

When the barn came into view, Mariam felt a shiver up her spine. Were the souls of all those barley harvesters in that barn, or in the caves where they died, or had they flown to heaven? She said a quick prayer for them, and then another as they passed by the spot where she and her family had camped out in the open.

Amina Hanim followed Mariam's gaze to the spot that held so many memories. "You'll all stay with us in the house," she said firmly. "You are like family now."

When the two-storey house came into view, Mariam noticed that it didn't look as prosperous as it did before. The garden was overgrown with weeds and there was an indefinable uncared-for quality about the place.

Instead of leaving them outside like Abdul Hassan had before, Amina Hanim motioned them to follow her into the house. They paused just inside the threshold, not knowing what to do.

Mariam had never been in a Turkish home before and was curious. The central room was clutter-free and almost totally devoid of furniture except for a low table and a number of large cushions on the floor. There were closed doors on either side of the main entrance. Mariam guessed that one door led to the men's quarters, and the other to the women's — although why they needed that when there were just the two of them was beyond her. There was also a set of stairs leading up to the second storey.

"Please sit down," said Amina Hanim, indicating the cushions on the floor, then she hurried out into the kitchen. Abdul Hassan sat down with his guests.

They had barely settled down into the cushions when she came back, bearing a platter of bread, olives, and cheese, which she set on the table. She scurried out again, and then moments later came back with a tall pitcher of water and clay tumblers.

"My apologies for the simple fare," she said. "My days are spent in the field." She set the pitcher and tumblers next to the tray and then stood over by the doorway.

"Sit with us, wife," said Abdul Hassan. "There are things we need to discuss."

A faint smile fluttered across her face, then she sat down on a cushion close to her husband.

Once their guests had eaten, Abdul Hassan said, "You cannot walk to Marash. I would take you right now, but my crop is going to seed."

Mariam nodded in understanding, anticipating what he was about to say.

"If you stay with us and help us get in as much of the crop as we can before it goes completely to seed, I shall pay you."

Mariam was about to open her mouth. Payment wasn't what they wanted. The Turk held up his hand for silence. "I will also take you myself to Marash. In my oxcart. God willing."

Mariam smiled. "Thank you," she said. The turn of events came as a relief. She had felt uneasy about travelling by foot all the way to Marash, but she hadn't been able to see an alternative. Just as her gut had told her in the spring that it was wrong to stay in this house then, now it was telling her this was the best choice.

Her one concern was for Anna. Could she work in the fields in her condition? And would the Turkish couple let her live in their house, or would their superstitions exile her to the barn? Mariam regarded Abdul

Hassan. This time he had barely taken notice of Anna. She looked over to Amina Hanim. The woman was staring at Anna. It was obvious that she wanted to ask a question, but didn't know how.

Anna, who always kept her eyes cast down in the presence of strangers, felt the heat of the gaze. She looked up and met Amina Hanim's eyes. "Yes?" she asked.

Amina Hanim quickly looked away. Looking at her own hands, which were rough and reddened with work, she said, "Hanim, can you work in the sun with your white skin?"

Mariam smiled inwardly. The very thing she was wondering herself.

"It is difficult," she said. "The sun burns my skin rapidly." She looked at Kevork, then Onnig, Marta, and Mariam. "But I would do anything to help these children."

"I can think of two possible solutions," said Amina Hanim. "You could stay inside and look after the house. That would free me up to work in the fields."

Anna nodded.

"You could also look after the little boy." Amina Hanim gestured towards Onnig.

"But that would be a waste of an adult," said Anna.

"Which leads me to my other possible solution," said Amina Hanim. "You would be hot, but a thick paste of oil and clay might protect your skin. I have used it myself when the sun's rays burn brightly."

"If the woman goes into the field," asked Abdul Hassan, "who will look after the boy?"

"I could," said Marta.

Everyone turned in her direction. "I am almost eight, and Onnig is my little brother. I know how to look after him."

"But could you look after the house while everyone else is in the field?" asked Amina Hanim.

"I have watched my sister and Anna bake bread," the little girl replied gravely. "I think I could do it. And I already know how to sweep and to wash clothing and many other household chores."

Mariam smiled sadly at this exchange. Her little sister had grown up quickly since their parents died. She could wash clothing, sweep, shell nuts, milk the goat, collect eggs, weed the garden, and many, many other things. The only reason she had never made flatbread was that she and Anna had made several weeks' worth at once, then dried it and stored it, taking out only what was needed each day.

"There would be no need for you to make Armenian flatbread," said Amina Hanim. "I make Turkish pide each morning before going to the fields."

The first time Mariam slashed her mother's tiny sickle through an expanse of wheat, an image of Turks with bayonets on horseback filled her mind. The thought gave her energy, and she pretended the stalks of wheat were her parents' killers. She slashed through them with a force she didn't realize she had.

"You're very good at this for such a young girl," said Amina Hanim, who was working not far from her.

If only she knew what I was thinking, mused Mariam.

Kevork was good at it too, and Mariam suspected that his thoughts were not much different from hers. Anna, on the other hand, had difficulty with the job. Although she was older than Mariam, she did not have the same strength, and the mud paste that she had to wear on her face and neck and hands made her exhausted with heat. After just a few hours, Anna sat down in the middle of the field. She tried to hold her face in her hands, but ended up smearing the mud concoction into her eyes and making them sting with the grit. She brought her knees close to her chest and hugged them tightly, smearing yet more mud.

"I feel so useless," she said.

Mariam came to sit beside her for a moment.

"Even you children are stronger than I am," said Anna. "What good am I to you?"

"You are like a mother to us," said Mariam. She took a corner of her veil and moistened it with her mouth, and then she carefully blotted the muddy mixture away from Anna's eyes. Mariam felt badly for Anna. What must it be like for her to be living with this handicap? She couldn't shed her white skin, and she couldn't change her strange sore eyes or the way that people reacted to her. The experiences of the last few months had made Anna more bitter than the others, yet she tried to rein it in for the sake of the children.

As Mariam considered Anna and her situation, her eyes wandered down to the sickle that Anna had been using. No wonder she was having so much difficulty. It was long and sharp, but very heavy. Mariam reached down and picked it up. It was easily twice as heavy as the precious one that she was using.

"Would you like to use my sickle for awhile?" suggested Mariam. She didn't really like to have her mother's tiny sickle out of her grasp, but Anna's need was greater than hers.

Anna looked at Mariam with gratitude. "You would lend it to me?" she asked.

"I don't have to be covered up like you, so I'm cooler," said Mariam. "Besides," she added in her most convincing voice, "I think I might prefer a heavier one for a bit."

Anna grinned. Mariam tried not to chuckle at the strange sight of Anna: white teeth and pink-rimmed blue eyes shining through a mud-streaked face.

Marta's first day of work wasn't as gruelling as it was for those in the fields, but it wasn't exactly easy, either. She set Onnig to work weeding the garden as she peeled onions to add to the pot of vegetable stew that Amina Hanim had put on the roof to cook in the sun before leaving for the fields. Amina had also asked Marta to thinly slice a basket of apples and lay the slices out on the roof to dry. Marta could not do either of these tasks very efficiently. She started with the onions because chopping was easier than slicing, and she didn't have to use such a sharp knife. Her eyes streamed with tears as she peeled away the skins, and her nose got extremely itchy while she chopped them. She couldn't wait to finish so she could wash her hands and give her nose a good scratching.

She decided to peel and slice the apples outside so she could keep a better eye on Onnig. He was intently digging a hole with a stick in a bare patch of the garden, but she didn't know how long this would amuse him. She brought out a small carpet to sit on, and a wooden cutting board and a bowl for the apples. Amina Hanim had shown her which knife was the best for the apples, and it looked formidably sharp.

She stuck her tongue out of the corner of her mouth and frowned in concentration as she tried to peel the first apple. Her mother had always made the apple peel a single long coil, but how? Marta held the knife and apple at arm's length. She didn't want to get it too close because she was afraid of cutting herself, but her peel came off in chunks instead of a thin ribbon. When she looked at the first peeled apple, she sighed in frustration. There was more peel and core than apple. Oh well, she would get better.

"Can I have some?" asked Onnig, as he came over from the garden to see what Marta was doing.

"You can eat these peels," she said, handing him the juicy chunks.

Onnig grinned and stuffed them into his mouth.

For the second apple, Marta held it a little bit closer. Her ribbons of peel were less fleshy, and they were a hand's length long.

"These ones don't taste so good," said Onnig disapprovingly. "I'll give them to Sevo and Tipi."

"That's a good idea," said Marta.

Sevo was grazing at the side of the house, her rope attached, but not tethered. Tipi, Abdul's goat, was grazing a few feet away from her.

Marta was lost in concentration with her apple peeling. By the fourth apple she was pleased with how easily she was able to peel an apple and still have something left to slice. She didn't think she'd ever master the one long peel, though.

As she finished peeling and coring and slicing each apple, she would place the slices in the bowl. When she was all done, she carried the bowl into the kitchen and squeezed a wedge of lemon over them, and then she carried the bowl up two flights of stairs to the roof.

The roof was flat and made of dirt that had hardened in the sun to a smooth gloss. She sat down and spread her skirt to one side and carefully placed a single layer of apple slices in rows starting at the edge of the roof.

While she was doing this, Marta looked over the edge to check on Onnig. He was feeding the last of the apple peels and cores to the goats and grinning ear to ear.

She went back to her work and laid out all of the apple slices. By the time she was done, she had covered a large square patch of the roof. She stood up and stretched, proud of a job well done, then shaded her eyes from the sun and looked out into the fields. She could see the rhythmic rise and fall of the sickles in the fields, but as far as she could tell, not much progress was being made. In the spring, Abdul Hassan had hired twenty or more strong male workers. Their little group was barely making a dent.

She looked beyond the fields towards the cave grave, but couldn't see it from her vantage point. She willed herself to remember her parents' faces, but she couldn't. "Please God," she whispered, "look after Mommy and Daddy and Uncle Aram."

Then she turned towards Marash. What would they find there? She hoped that her grandmother and aunt and cousins were still alive.

From where she stood, she could see the old stone bridge that crossed over the Jihan River at Adana. She could also see the ancient castle in the distance. Looking at them again from this vantage point reminded her of the first time she had seen them. She had been such a child then, yet it was only a couple of months ago.

She took one last look down to the garden, but Onnig wasn't there. "Onnig?" she called. No answer.

She scurried down the stairs as quickly as she could and ran out the front door of the house. "Onnig?" she called. "Where are you?"

Her heart beating in her throat, she ran around to the back of the house. There was Onnig, with Sevo and the other goat. His hands were tangled in their ropes and they were pulling him harder than he could hold them.

"Help!" he said to his sister, a frightened look in his eyes.

"What are you doing?" she asked, grabbing Sevo's rope firmly in one hand. With the tension off the rope, Onnig had no troubling untangling one of his hands. Marta then steadied Tipi by holding that rope firmly so Onnig could get free.

"They wanted to go to Marash," said Onnig. "But I didn't know they would go so fast."

Marta smiled. "We'll all be going to Marash soon, Onnig, but next time the goats want to go, tell them they'll have to wait."

The evening meal was served in the common main room of the house. Amina Hanim carried the pot of stew from the roof, and Marta walked in behind her, a serious frown on her face, carrying a platter of pide. Everyone took a wedge of the bread and then dipped it, a piece at a time, into the communal pot.

Once they had all eaten their fill, Amina Hanim and Marta took what was left back to the kitchen. Abdul Hassan leaned back on his cushion and smiled.

"Thank you for your help today," he said. His eyes rested briefly first on Kevork, then Mariam, and finally on Anna.

Anna had cleaned the mud from her skin, and her pale complexion had a sore pink glow to it. There were bluish shadows under her red-rimmed eyes, but she smiled back at the Turk. "It is our pleasure to help you," she said. "Will you be taking the threshed wheat to Marash?"

"I will," he said. "I was there a few weeks ago, and whatever I can bring will be sold for a good price. All over Adana, the wheat is being left unharvested."

Anna opened her mouth as if to reply, but then closed it again.

"Were you going to say something?" asked Abdul Hassan.

"No," said Anna.

Mariam looked from one to the other. She knew what Anna was about to say: had the Armenians not been killed, there wouldn't be this crisis now.

"Did it ever occur to you that I might agree with what you have to say?" Abdul Hassan asked Anna, with a touch of impatience in his voice. "It was wrong for the Sultan to initiate the massacres. He has been charged with his crimes and he has been deposed."

Mariam's mouth opened slightly with surprise.

"Killing Armenians makes as much sense as Mother Turkey chopping off her right hand," said Abdul Hassan. "We will all be paying for this for a long time."

Amina Hanim had come back from the kitchen and was standing in the doorway with Marta beside her. The look on her face showed that she was not comfortable with the turn in conversation. "Should I serve the coffee, Abdul-Agha?" she asked gently.

He turned towards her and frowned, but when he noticed her expression, his annoyance softened. "Yes wife," he said. "That would be fine."

After coffee and conversation on more neutral topics, it was time to go to bed.

Amina Hanim opened one of the doors off the common room and said, "Ladies, follow me."

Marta looked at Mariam with a question in her eyes, and Mariam returned with a look that meant, "Do as you're told." The girls stepped towards the door with Anna.

"Take me with you," said Onnig.

"Our haremlik is small," said Amina Hanim to the little boy. "Can't you sleep with Kevork and my husband in the salemlik?"

"Why can't we all sleep together in this room?" asked Onnig, pointing to all the cozy pillows on the floor.

Amina Hassan smiled indulgently. The concept was entirely foreign to her. "What an interesting idea, child." Then she looked at Kevork. "He'll be all right with you, won't he?"

Kevork nodded. "He'll be fine."

Mariam didn't know what to expect when she stepped through the door to the haremlik, but it certainly wasn't what she found. It was made up of just one plain room, and there were ledges built into the walls on all four sides. Two walls of the ledges were lined with Turkish carpets, and the other two were bare. In the middle of the room was a tonir sunk into the floor, with cushions around it.

"It is cool enough tonight that you might want to sleep by the warmth of the tonir," said Amina Hanim, "but if you prefer, you can sleep by the wall."

Mariam and Marta cuddled up together on pillows beside the tonir. Anna slept beside them, and Amina Hanim chose a spot against the wall.

Had Kevork been able to compare, he would have realized that the salemlik was much more carefully furnished than the haremlik. Abdul Hassan had two rooms to himself. One of the rooms had an elaborate carpet on the floor with richly embroidered cushions on top. In the centre of the room was a *hookah* — a water pipe used to smoke tobacco — and in one corner was a prayer mat facing Mecca. Even the walls in this room were hung with beautiful Turkish carpets. It was divided from the second room by a doorway of beads. This second room of the salemlik was similar to the haremlik's single room, although the cushions were more heavily embroidered.

Abdul ushered Kevork and Onnig to the tonir in the main room. "This is where you shall sleep," he said. Then he pushed aside the beaded divider and stepped into the other room.

As Kevork settled in to sleep, he could see the silhouette of Abdul on his knees, bowing towards Mecca. The rhythmic sound of prayers drifted through the beads.

They worked the fields for three weeks, but did not manage to harvest even a third of the wheat before it dried on the stalks.

"Because of the decimation of so many fields, even this small yield will bring in a fair price," said Abdul Hassan with satisfaction as they gathered together for what was supposed to be a final evening meal.

Mariam saw him look at her with an appraising eye. What must I look like to him? she wondered. As she reached for a fig and popped it in her mouth, she saw how her arms had changed. They were now brown as a nut and faintly muscular, but they looked more womanly than girlish. She looked up and caught his eye. He returned the look with a fatherly glance of approval. She was glad they were leaving soon. She had a feeling that he would like nothing better than to marry her off to some young Turk.

She watched as he appraised the others in her group, and she did the same, trying to imagine how they must all appear from his point of view. Kevork's shoulders had broadened with hard work and he looked more like a little man than a boy. Mariam thought Abdul probably wouldn't mind keeping Kevork around as a farm hand.

When Abdul Hassan's appraising gaze fell on Anna, Mariam was pleased to see that his face held nothing but affection and respect. Anna's face was a painful blistered red, and her hands were cracked and callused. The issue of the Evil Eye seemed moot.

Mariam already knew how both Abdul Hassan and his wife felt about Onnig. On more than one occasion they had mentioned that they would love to adopt him. Amina had confided in Mariam that they had lost both of their sons. One had died in infancy, and the other had died as a soldier in the Sultan's army. Amina could no longer have children, and she had suggested to her husband that he take on a second wife, but he refused.

Mariam also knew how they both felt about Marta. She turned to look at her now. As always, she was close to the skirts of Amina. With the veil tucked tightly over her hair and a small apron over her dress, she looked like a miniature version of a Turkish housewife. Mariam knew that Amina had come to depend on her.

Abdul Hassan drew a purse of coins from his belt and turned to Mariam. "As promised, here is your payment." He handed the purse to her.

"Thank you," said Mariam with a smile. "This will help us when we get to Marash."

The Turk replied, "So you are truly set on leaving?"

"Where else would we go?"

"Let me be frank," said Abdul Hassan. "The Armenians in Marash fared much better than those in Adana. In fact, some Turks even hid their Armenian neighbours when the gendarmes rained down with their bayonets."

"That is good to know," said Mariam.

"However," said Abdul Hassan, "Marash is not entirely safe. The Young Turks have grasped power from the Sultan and some say they are even more fanatical than he was."

"But I thought they believed in reforming Turkey," said Mariam.

"They do," replied Abdul Hassan, "but not in the way you mean. They believe Turkey is for Turks, and no one else. Even now, there are rumblings against the minorities."

Mariam sighed in frustration. "Armenians have lived in this area for more than two thousand years. Where are they supposed to go?"

Abdul was silent for a moment. It was as if he wanted to say something, but didn't quite know how.

"There is a way," he said. "I could take you in. I would adopt the boy and maybe the girl," he said, gesturing first at Onnig, then at Marta. "And Anna, you are welcome to stay in our home. I could find a husband for you, Mariam, and a job for Kevork."

"You mean we would become Turkish?" asked Mariam.

"There are worse fates," replied Abdul Hassan dryly.

"We cannot change who we are," said Mariam, "and I for one would rather die Armenian than live as a Turk."

A look of utter shock passed over Abdul Hassan's face. He was silent for a moment, struggling for words. Then he said, "As you wish. But please remember that I tried to help."

CHAPTER SIX

By dawn the next morning, the sturdy oxcart with huge wooden wheels was packed tightly with sacks of wheat and the meagre possessions of Anna and the children. Mariam was pleased that their provisions for the trip — dried meat, goat cheese, barley soaked in yogurt, dried apples, and raisins — had mostly been prepared by her little sister.

The children bid Amina Hanim goodbye with teary smiles. "May Allah save you from the worst," she said.

There was only room for two people in the cart at a time, so they rotated, with Onnig invariably sitting on someone's lap. Sevo walked behind, her rope tethered to the frame of the cart.

As they walked through the mighty gates of Marash, Mariam's heart thumped with joy. It felt so good to be on safe ground. Abdul Hassan insisted on taking them directly to their grandmother's house.

As the oxcart creaked down the cobblestone streets, Mariam drank in the sights. The covered bazaar was bursting with colour and noise as Armenians and Turks, Kurds and Arabs, Greeks and Jews all haggled over prices as if the massacres had never happened. Mariam inhaled deeply the old familiar smells of Marash: fresh coffee, fruit, different kinds of baking bread. Below these powerful aromas there was a faint smell of something rotting.

She felt excited, but also a bit apprehensive. Would her grandmother and aunt still be alive? She was too impatient to sit in the oxcart, so she hopped down and walked beside Abdul Hassan. Without even needing directions, he had been guiding the ox towards the Armenian section.

"It's down this way," said Mariam, walking a few steps in front of Abdul. With the oxcart they couldn't take the shortcut and had to stick to the wider roads.

"We're almost there," said Mariam with a grin, darting between other travellers.

Then, before she knew it, Mariam was standing at the street wall in front of her own house. It seemed smaller than she had remembered it, and somehow shabbier.

The last time she had been here, the wall in front of the courtyard had been well over her head. Now she could see over top of it when she stood on tiptoes. She grinned at the familiar sight of the apricot, fig, and almond trees. She spied her own goat, Lala, whose pale yellow coat with a dark brown patch on her neck was as familiar to Mariam as the back of her own hand. She also saw Yar, her grandmother's goat, and several chickens.

There was an old-fashioned bell on a chain above the garden door, and Mariam pulled the rope with all her might, giggling at the sound of the familiar clang. There was no answer. She pulled it again. No answer.

"Mariam, look in the window," Kevork said.

Mariam got back up on her tiptoes and looked over the wall. There was a small glass-covered window beside the front door of the house, and she could see someone peering through it. She realized that her grandmother must have been scared out of her wits, seeing Abdul Hassan, Kevork, and Anna with the cart.

"Grandmother, it's me," she called. "Onnig and Marta are here, too! Please open the door."

Mariam jumped and flailed her arms, and Marta stood up in the cart, and she held Onnig up so he could wave.

Suddenly, the door opened wide. There stood Anahid Baji — Grandmother Hovsepian — looking older than Mariam remembered. Her hair had been steel grey, but now it was completely white. And there were lines of worry on her forehead that hadn't been there when Mariam had kissed her goodbye a lifetime ago.

The look in Anahid Baji's eyes was one of incomprehension. "I thought you were dead," she whispered, her hand covering her mouth. "Word came that all the harvesters were killed."

There was a shuffling sound behind Anahid Baji, then another woman stood beside her. This was Aram's widow, Aunt Ovsanna. She was a head taller than Anahid Baji, and thin like a reed. Mariam had never noticed it before, but she had a faint resemblance to her own dead mother. When Ovsanna recognized her nieces and nephew, her knees buckled, and she crumpled to the ground. Mariam stretched her arm over the gate and unlatched the hook, then she ran to Ovsanna and helped her up. "It's okay," she said. "We couldn't get back sooner."

"Is Aram dead?"

"He is," said Mariam, hugging her aunt tight. "We gave him a proper burial."

"Thank God at least for that," said Aunt Ovsanna, crossing herself. "May his soul rest in heaven."

Anahid Baji stood, her eyes taking in the scene before her — Ovsanna in Mariam's arms, Marta and Onnig in the cart with strangers — and the news tumbling out that both of her sons had indeed been killed. Her eyes filled with tears. "My sons," she said. "Both dead. And my dear daughter-in-law too. Thanks be to God that you children survived."

Marta tumbled out of the oxcart, then helped Onnig down. They both ran to their grandmother, hugging her skirts and weeping.

By this time, Ovsanna's two children had come to the door to see what the commotion was. Gadar was two years younger than her cousin Marta, but the two looked like sisters. Her younger brother, Aram, was the same age as Onnig. Aram and Gadar hadn't seen their cousins for awhile, and so they stood just inside the threshold, looking shyly on.

Another person who felt less than comfortable was Abdul Hassan. He stood awkwardly beside the oxcart, his hand tightly gripping the rope, and his face flushed bright red.

Kevork, too, didn't know where to look or what to do, so he stayed in the cart and looked down at his hands. Anna sat beside him. She reached over and gripped one of his hands.

Mariam came to her senses first. "We have friends with us," she announced.

Mariam watched Ovsanna's expression as she looked in confusion from the burly Turk, to the boy, and then to the strange-looking woman. Mariam gripped her by the hand and led her to the oxcart. She looked behind her and saw that Anahid Baji had one of her hands in Marta's and another in Onnig's, and they were pulling her towards the cart too.

Anahid Baji couldn't quite hide the hostility in her eyes when she came face to face with Abdul Hassan. He bowed politely to her, while her eyes darted from him to Mariam in confusion.

"Grandmother, I would like to introduce you to our dear friend, Abdul Hassan. This gentleman and his wife fed us and housed us and treated us like family. To ensure our safety, he travelled with us in his own oxcart from Adana right to your doorstep."

The hostility on Anahid Baji's face dissolved in an instant. She returned Abdul's bow and said, "You are a good man. God bless you. Thank you for looking after my children."

Mariam said, "Grandmother, there are two other people I would like you to meet. They have become our second family." She reached up her hand and helped Anna down from the oxcart.

"This is Anna Adomian," said Mariam. "And Anna,

this is my dear grandmother, Anahim Hovsepian, and my aunt, Ovsanna Hovsepian."

Anna looked at the old woman quickly, then lowered her eyes, her cheeks flushing with embarrassment. She bowed to the old woman. Then she turned to Ovsanna and, without raising her eyes, bowed again.

Anahid Baji let go of Marta and Onnig's hands and walked over to Anna and took her hand. "Sister Anna," she said, "welcome to our humble home."

Onnig ran over to the side of the oxcart and called up to Kevork, "Come down, come down. You've got to meet my family!"

Kevork looked down at the little boy's excited face and was pleased to see such happy enthusiasm. When had he seen Onnig so happy before? Never. But the boy's happiness and the whole homecoming scene had made Kevork even more intensely aware of all that he had lost. Were his parents dead? How would be ever know if they were dead or alive, now that he had abandoned his home to travel to Marash. He smiled faintly at the little boy, then stood up and hopped down from the cart.

Onnig gripped his hand tightly and pulled him forward.

"Grandmother," said Onnig, his eyes flashing with delight. "This is Kevork. He's my big brother now."

Kevork blushed with embarrassment, then bowed deeply to the elderly woman. "I am Kevork Adomian, Anna's nephew," explained Kevork.

Anahid Baji looked from the loving sparkle in her grandson's eyes to Kevork's forlorn ones. She had an idea that this boy had lost much, but he had still found love to give to her grandson. Instead of bowing to him as Kevork had expected, Anahid Baji stepped forward and hugged him with all her might. She was older than his mother — much older — and he never knew his grandmother. But there was something in her scent and her ways that reminded him of his mother. Enveloped in her arms, he broke out into convulsive sobs. The sadness that he had been holding in for so long had unexpectedly broken forth.

Anahid Baji hugged him harder and rocked him in her arms. "You've lost so much," she whispered hoarsely, "but we're your family, too."

CHAPTER SEVEN

It was weeks later when Anna came up with a plan.
She stepped out into the garden looking for Kevork,
but he wasn't there. She climbed the ladder that went up
onto the roof. When she poked her head out, she found
him sitting with Marta and the younger children, playing a game with pebbles.

"Nephew," she said.

Kevork looked up from his game.

"Can you walk with me?" she asked.

By the way that she said it, Kevork knew not to
argue. He looked over at Marta, Onnig, and the cousins.
"You're in charge, Marta," he said with a wink.

Anna took the veil that rested around her shoulders and drew it over her head, then wrapped the ends
loosely around her neck to cover the bottom half of
her face.

Instead of going down the ladder, Anna walked to
the southern edge and stepped onto the next roof.

Kevork followed her. She and Kevork were used to getting around in their old village this way, and so it came as second nature to travel this way in Marash, too. You could get practically all the way from one end of the city to the other by stepping from roof to roof. There were a few two-storey buildings that got in the way, and every once in awhile the space between the roofs required more of a hop than a step, but it was much quicker travelling by rooftop if you were going by foot. No need to dart out of the way of horses and oxcarts.

Kevork fell in beside his aunt. "Where are we going?" he asked.

"To the Church of the Forty Sainted Youths," said Anna, holding her skirt away from her feet with one hand and her veil in place with the other. "The rectory, not the church."

"Why?" asked Kevork. His aunt had such a serious expression on her face that he frowned with worry.

"I need to talk to the Vartabed," she explained. "I am hoping he can advise me."

"But why him?" asked Kevork.

"Because he's the only person in Marash that I know," said Anna.

Kevork followed her in silence. The Church of the Forty Sainted Youths was south of the Armenian district, close to the city gates. He had a fairly good idea what she needed advice on. It was obvious that Anahid Baji was running out of funds, and that their household was simply too big to manage. Mariam had turned over her purse of coins to her grandmother, but even that was being emptied at an alarmingly fast rate. If Anna had a way of resolving this situation, he would do anything he could to help her.

As they stepped from rooftop to rooftop, Anna and Kevork nodded at others who walked past them in their own travels. They also gingerly stepped around people's cooking pots and fruits drying in the sun. Once, they startled a Turkish boy who was in such deep concentration navigating his kite that he didn't hear the footsteps on his roof.

"Ack!" the boy said, momentarily loosening his grip on the wooden cross that he used to manoeuvre the kite strings.

Kevork stopped for a moment and looked in the air. The boy's kite was in the shape of a huge dove with outspread wings. It was glittering white silk with edging in mauve and grey. The sight brought a sudden catch to Kevork's throat, as he thought of the simple white bird kite that his father had made for him. He looked at the boy and realized they were probably the same age. But this boy had an innocence about him that Kevork had long ago left behind.

"Sorry," said Kevork, with a faint smile. Then he added, "That is a beautiful kite."

The boy looked up and grinned.

A few rooftops after the boy with the kite, there appeared a row of two-storey houses.

"Can you help me down?"

Kevork hopped down from the lower sloped side of the last single-storey roof, then reached up and helped his aunt down to the ground.

"We're almost there," she said, pointing down the street at a solid-looking building with a cone-shaped roof topped with a cross. "The rectory is beside it."

When they got there, Anna knocked gingerly on the rear door of the rectory. It was answered by a stooped Armenian woman dressed in black.

"Is the Very Reverend Vartabed Garabed in?" asked Anna.

"Does the Vartabed know you?" asked the housekeeper, looking Kevork and Anna up and down with suspicion.

"Not to see," replied Anna. "But he knows my name. I corresponded with him when I was Father Dikran's secretary."

"Oh," said the woman, crossing herself. "Poor Father Dikran. So many deaths, a church destroyed." The old woman opened the door all the way. "Come in. I'll tell Father Garabed he has visitors."

They followed her through the kitchen, then down a central corridor to a room at the front of the house. Kevork's nose wrinkled at the mustiness of the place. This woman may have been the housekeeper, but it didn't look like she was much of one. There was a sagging wooden bookcase against one wall, and two other walls were covered with Armenian carpets. Kevork noted that they had once been beautiful like the ones his mother made, but they were now faded and dusty with age. The remaining wall had a small window grimed with dust, and there was a crucifix nailed above it. A heavy wooden desk dominated the room, and there were several uncomfortable-looking wooden chairs facing the desk.

The woman gestured for them to sit down. "Father Garabed will be here shortly," she said.

A few minutes later, a tall, gangly man entered the room. He wasn't very old, and while he was dressed in a priest's black cap and robe, he didn't have a beard. Kevork had never seen a priest without a beard before. Kevork stood up and bowed his head in reverence.

Anna stood up, then knelt before the priest, kissing his hand. "God be your helper, Very Reverend Father."

"Bless you, child." He helped her back up to her feet. "Are you Anna Adomian?"

"Yes," said Anna. "And this is my nephew, Kevork."

Kevork stepped forward, then knelt in front of the priest just as Anna had done.

The priest accepted Kevork's greeting, then extended his hand, helping him back to his feet. He gathered up the skirts of his cassock and perched at the edge of the desk. "Make yourselves comfortable," said the priest, indicating the chairs.

Kevork and Anna sat back down.

"Why did you come to me?" he asked.

"I need a job," said Anna. "I can read and write. I can sew and cook."

Kevork looked at his aunt. The hopelessness of the situation was clear. How could one woman possibly make enough money to feed five children and three adults? He looked at the priest's expression and saw that his thoughts were similar. If he only knew, thought Kevork. It is not just me that Anna wants to support.

The priest was quiet for a moment, and then he said, "There are a few possibilities."

Kevork saw Anna's shoulders relax just a bit, and a look of hopeful anticipation formed on her face.

"Did you know that there is an orphanage in Marash run by the Near East Relief?"

Anna's shoulders sagged. "I am not going to put Kevork in an orphanage."

The priest said nothing.

Anna continued, "Kevork is not my only concern. There are four other children and two other women."

The priest frowned. "These are all survivors of the Adana massacre?"

"No," said Anna. "They are from Marash, but their family was killed with the barley harvesters who had travelled to Marash, and now they have no means of support."

"You are not the first who has come to me with a sad story," said the Vartabed.

Kevork could see that the priest's face was troubled, but that he was struggling to remain firm.

"The orphanage could help," said the priest. "The missionaries are good people."

"But these children have lost so much already," said Anna. "Is there not a way that I could get a job and support them?"

The priest looked at her with troubled eyes. "Dear sister Anna," he said, "who would hire you? People are superstitious. Being a woman is hard enough, but a woman with your affliction — that makes it impossible."

Kevork could see tears well up in his aunt's eyes. He didn't know if they were tears of anger or sadness, but he suspected they were of anger. His aunt was one of the most determined people he knew.

"You must help me," Anna said fiercely. "These children must stay together, and I will do everything possible to make that happen."

"Let me see what I can do," said the priest.

Anna and Kevork walked back to the Hovsepian household in silence.

A week later, early one morning, the bell at the door in the street wall chimed.

Ovsanna hurried to answer it, then ushered their guest into the courtyard. "Please wait here for one moment," she said excitedly.

"Anna Adomian, there is a priest here to see you." Ovsanna could barely contain her curiosity as she stepped back into the main room. She found Anna just as she had left her. Anna had folded up the bed linens and propped them up against the storage space built into the wall. She was in the midst of rearranging the heavy carpet that hung from the ceiling and draped over the bedding, hiding it for the daytime and creating space in the room for daily activities.

Since Anna had arrived, this was one daily ritual that she had taken over. In her home village, everyone slept around the tonir, and she was fascinated with the bed that went into the wall and disappeared during the day.

Anna quickly tucked in the last sleeping pillow behind the wall carpet. "Do I look all right?" she asked

Ovsanna, straightening her hair and smoothing down the front of her dress.

"You look fine," said Ovsanna with a smile. "I will show him in."

Anna stood nervously clasping her hands in front of her as Ovsanna ushered the priest in. He was so tall that he had to bend his head to walk through the door.

She knelt before him. "God be your helper, Very Reverend Father."

"Bless you, child," he said, then helped her to her feet.

Anna looked up to the priest's face and she saw that his kind eyes sparkled with excitement. "I have good news for you," he said.

Anna's heart pounded with anticipation. So he had found a job for her after all? That would be such welcome news to the household. She didn't know how much longer they would be able to last. However, she knew it was rude to ask him his news before she had offered him hospitality.

"Please sit," she said, indicating a richly embroidered cushion close to the fireplace.

The priest sat down, a smile on his face.

"I shall make us some coffee," she said. Then with trembling hands, she walked to the shelf and took down the coffee grinder, then poured in a measure of beans. As she cranked the handle and breathed in the aromatic blend, her heart beat in anticipation.

Anna filled the long-handled pot with water and set it on the metal platform in the fireplace to boil. As the water heated, she turned to smile at the priest.

"I have spoken to the administrator at the orphanage about you," he said.

Anna's smile began to crumple. She was about to respond but stopped, afraid she would say the wrong thing.

"You can live there," the Vartabed continued. "They will give you room and board and a small fee each week."

Anna could feel tears forming in her eyes. She thought she had explained to the Vartabed that the family could not be split up. She knew the Vartabed was being kind, but didn't he realize that she couldn't live at the orphanage? Who would look after Kevork? And what about Marta, Mariam, and Onnig? And what about Anahim Baji, Ovsanna, and the children? Her small fee couldn't possibly support them all, and besides, she would be torn from them. This didn't seem like a solution at all.

"Is there something the matter?" asked the Vartabed.

A tear rolled down Anna's cheek, and she wiped it angrily away. "I can't be separated from these children," she said.

The Vartabed grinned. "I know that." He reached forward and took Anna's hand. "That's the best part: Josefine Younger, the orphanage administrator, has agreed to let you bring Kevork with you."

Anna was about to say something, but the Vartabed held up his hand. "Marta and Mariam and Onnig are welcome too. If they would like to go."

"But they have family here," said Anna.

"Many of the children at the orphanage have some family living," replied the priest. "And they can visit on

Sundays. But in the meantime, the children will be given an education, and food and lodging."

Anna was silent as she considered the idea.

"You will have no expenses, and yet Miss Younger will pay you a small weekly fee."

Anna could tell by the way he said it that this was an arrangement he had gone to great lengths to make.

"It is not much money, but it will help the ones who stay in this house."

Vartabed Garabed was silent as he waited for Anna to say something. She had completely forgotten about the boiling pot of water, and it would have boiled dry, except Ovsanna had slipped in quietly. She sat down beside Anna and wordlessly made the coffee, handing a demitasse to the priest and another to Anna. She was about to get up and leave, but Anna reached out and placed her hand on Ovsanna's forearm.

"Stay," she said.

So Ovsanna sat back down.

After a minute or more of silence, Anna asked, "Did Miss Younger say what she would be hiring me to do?"

"She wants to meet you before making a firm decision."

"Will the children be able to stay together?" Anna asked.

"The girls will be together at Bethel and the boys will be at Beitshalom."

"How soon are we to leave?"

"As soon as you wish," said the Vartabed Garabed.

"The children will need time to adjust to the idea," said Anna.

"Of course," said the priest. "A few days will not make a difference." He blew on his coffee, then drained it in a single gulp. "This will be the best for all," he said. Then he handed the empty demitasse to Ovsanna and stood up.

Anna and Ovsanna stood up too and walked him to the door, then through the courtyard to the gate.

When the gate clicked shut behind him, Ovsanna turned to Anna, angry tears in her eyes. "What are you thinking?" she asked. "The children cannot go to an orphanage."

"We need to talk about it, all of us," said Anna. "This may be the only way for us to survive."

That evening, once dinner had been eaten and cleared away, and the bed had been pulled back down from behind the wall carpet, the family cuddled together in the dim light of the fireplace to talk about the day's events.

Ovsanna sat on a cushion leaning against the foot of the bed, with Onnig tucked in the crook of one arm, Gadar on her lap, and Aram in the crook of her other arm. "I think it is a good opportunity for you, Anna," she said, holding her children close.

Anna sat on the bed, her feet curled under her, directly behind Ovsanna. Kevork sat next to her, cross-legged and rigid, waiting to hear what his future would be.

In the middle of the bed sat Anahid Baji, her back propped up with pillows, and her granddaughters, Mariam and Marta, on either side.

"It could be a good opportunity for us all," said Anahid Baji.

Ovsanna tightened her embrace on the three children in her arms and replied, "What do you mean?"

"Did you know that the orphanage provides an education to their charges?" said Anahid Baji.

"I can teach my own children to read and write," said Ovsanna.

"But you can't teach them a trade," said Anahid Baji. "How will these children support themselves as they grow older?"

Ovsanna stayed silent in the darkness.

Anna cleared her throat, then said, "There is a more immediate problem, Mairig."

"What is that, child?" answered Anahid Baji.

"We have no source of income for the household," said Anna. "All of the coins, both yours and Mariam's, are nearly gone."

Anahid Baji was silent for a moment. What Anna said was true, but she didn't know the other woman realized it. "And how will your working at the orphanage resolve that problem?" she asked.

"Kevork and I are eating your food, but not contributing to the pot," said Anna. "My salary at the orphanage could be given to you as repayment for your kindness."

"You and Kevork are family now," said Anahid Baji. "What is mine is yours."

"And what is mine is yours," returned Anna. "There will be fewer mouths to feed, and the children will be educated."

"My children will not go to an orphanage," said Ovsanna fiercely.

"Your children are still young," said Anna.

"Onnig is also too young," said Ovsanna.

"Let us not argue," said Anahid Baji. "This is the way it shall be. Onnig and Aram and Gadar shall stay in this house. They are too young to go to school, and so there is no advantage for them at the orphanage."

Ovsanna let out a huge sigh of relief. "You are right, Mairig," she said. "They are too young."

"Mariam needs an education," said Anahid Baji, "and her sister should stay with her."

Mariam swallowed back a sob in the darkness. She knew her grandmother was right, but the prospect of living at an orphanage was terrifying. She felt her grandmother's hand grasp hers in the darkness and give it a reassuring squeeze. "You and Marta can always come back here if it doesn't work out," she said.

"We will give it a try," said Mariam in her bravest voice.

"What about me?" asked Kevork.

"You will be coming with me to the orphanage," said Anna firmly. "You need a trade, and I need you near me."

The family settled into silence after that, pondering their newly minted future. Mariam tried to hold back her sobs, but the thought of leaving her grandmother's house and all she held dear was too much for her. She bit the edge of her pillow and silently wept. Even more terrifying than leaving this home was the prospect of being separated from her baby brother. In her head, she knew that he was much better off staying with Ovsanna and her children, but her heart was breaking. One more part of her family was being torn away.

Mariam pasted a brave smile on her face as she and her sister walked towards the stone gate that circled the huge orphanage complex. Kevork and Anna were mere steps behind them, but everyone was silent in their own thoughts.

They stepped up to the street door, and then Mariam reached up and pulled a rope hanging from a bell at the top of the door. The bell rang once, and then the door opened just a crack.

Mariam's heart pounded wildly in her chest. Who would answer? And what did this place have in store for them?

"Who is it?" a small voice from the other side of the door asked.

Mariam peered through the crack, but didn't see anyone, but then her sister said, "Hello!"

Mariam looked down and saw one mischievous brown eye. Anna stepped forward. Crouching down so she could look into the eye, she said, "Miss Younger is expecting us. I am Anna Adomian."

The door opened wide. A little girl, perhaps five years old, with unkempt hair and a broad smile stood there. "My name is Paris. Mother Younger told me you'd be coming!"

Mariam's eyes widened as they stepped inside of the complex. It was huge. A city within a city. Directly in front of her was the kind of street Mariam had heard about in

England and France. It was straight and broad and paved with bricks. The buildings on either side of the road were made of the same kind of uniformly sized bricks as the road, and they were several storeys high. They had hundreds of windows of plain rectangular glass that reflected the sunlight. As far as Mariam's eyes could see, there was huge square building after huge square building. They looked cold and foreign, as far as she was concerned.

Paris gestured with her hand for them to follow her, and then she scampered down the street.

As the little group followed Paris down the street, Mariam was greeted with a number of sensations. She could hear voices floating from the buildings as she passed. She caught snippets of an arithmetic lesson, and then a flash of German grammar. Her nose wrinkled at a brief scent of chalk, and then of bread baking, and then of laundry soap. So much activity, yet no one in the street.

Paris walked up to one of the buildings and knocked on the door. It was opened by a foreign woman with yellow hair parted in the middle and pulled into a tight bun at the nape of her neck. She wore a Western-style long-sleeved white blouse and a plain black skirt.

"Thank you, Paris," the woman said, then patted the girl affectionately on the head. Paris scampered away. The woman turned towards them. "Welcome."

She regarded each of them individually with a smile, and then her eyes rested on Anna. "I've heard many good things about you, Miss Adomian."

Mariam was impressed by the fact that the missionary didn't react to Anna's unusual appearance.

"My name is Josefine Younger," said the woman, extending her hand to Anna. "Let us get these children settled, and then you and I shall talk over a cup of tea and we can decide what your role at the orphanage will be."

Mariam and Marta were given a place together in a long room with sleeping cots for a dozen or more girls. Kevork's place was in a building on the boys' side of the orphanage complex.

As the days and the weeks and the years flew by, Mariam came to cherish the comforting routine at the orphanage. In the beginning, she was a student, but as time rolled by, she stepped more and more into the role of a teacher. There seemed to be a never-ending trickle of Armenian orphans arriving each week, but nothing prepared her for 1915.

BOOK TWO

Chapter Eight

April 1915

In the shadowy darkness of the early morning, Mariam turned her head on her pillow and looked over at her sister, who was still fast asleep in the cot beside her. Marta's profile still had the softness of childhood, and her brow was untroubled. How Mariam would have loved to be able to keep that brow untroubled, but the rumours she'd been hearing lately let her know that Marta would be growing up all too soon.

Mariam sat up and rubbed the sleep out of her eyes, then threw off the bedcovers. She had to get up earlier than the others in her dorm room today, because it was her turn to prepare the bread-baking pit. It was too dark for her to see the row of cots, but the regular breathing and occasional mid-dream murmur told her that everyone else was still asleep. Not wanting to wake them, she didn't light a lantern. Instead, she got up and felt her way to the pitcher of water and basin that sat on a table at the far end of the room. She splashed her face with water, more to wake herself than for hygiene, then felt her way back to her cot. She straightened out the bedding, then slipped off her thin cotton nightgown and stuffed it under her pillow. Standing naked in the room of sleeping girls, Mariam looked down at her body, her eyes adjusting to the dim light. Unlike Marta, Mariam was no longer a child. Her breasts were full and her waist was slim. She had seen how men looked at her when she walked by and it embarrassed her.

Better to be childlike. Especially in these uncertain times.

She sighed.

Mariam opened up the wooden chest at the foot of her bed and took out her clothing. She quickly stepped into her orphanage-issue knee-length underwear, and then she took a long piece of thin cotton and wrapped it tightly around her breasts to minimize their curves. Then she pulled an undershirt over her head and drew on her long-sleeved white shirt. Before putting on her ankle-length grey skirt, she grabbed a pair of socks from the chest. These socks had been knitted by her aunt Ovsanna at the widows' charity. Shortly after she, Marta, Kevork, and Anna had come to live at the orphanage, the Vartabed had arranged for Ovsanna to earn some money by working for a few hours a day at a knitting mill making socks. The enterprise was run by the Armenian churches in Marash, and the socks were donated to the orphanage, but also sold in the bazaar.

Once she was fully dressed, Mariam reached underneath her bed and pulled out boots. Hers were in much better repair than her sister's, whose latest growth spurt had caused her toes to split the seams. Mariam had stopped growing two years earlier when she was fourteen, and so her boots were not too terribly abused.

She gave one last look at her sleeping sister, then headed out. The sun was just peeking over the mountain in the distance when Mariam stepped out onto the street. The air was fresh and cool, and she could hear the creaking of oxcarts and the howling of dogs beyond the orphanage walls. Marash was just starting to wake up.

Mariam pushed open the door to the kitchen and grabbed matches from the shelf, then stepped through the back door to where the covered baking pit was. The pit was enclosed in a little wooden shed with a tin roof. Mariam reached into the kindling bin at the side of the shed and drew out some dried grapevines. She stepped inside, then breathed in deeply the sweet smell of smoke and yeast that was a constant in the shed, even in the cold stillness of the morning.

The pit itself was about three feet deep and had a stone bottom and smooth stone sides. She threw the dried grapevines into the bottom of the pit and then lit them with a match. Once there was a good blaze, she threw on some thin sticks of wood, waited until they were burning steadily, and then added some sturdier ones. Her face got red with the heat, and she smiled with satisfaction as the flames settled into a lower, steadier glow. Now she had about an hour to wait until the wood turned to glowing embers.

She stepped back into the kitchen.

"Good morning, Mariam."

She caught her breath in surprise. Standing in the doorway was Rustem Bey, a full head taller than she was, but not much older. He wore a cream-coloured silk turban on his head, but was dressed in a European-style brown suit. He had burlap sacks of raisins and flour on the floor in front of him.

"Since when have you taken to being a delivery boy?" she asked.

"How else would I get to see you?" He smiled.

Mariam felt her face go hot with embarrassment. Rustem Bey was born to wealth, and unlike the rest of his family, he was known for his tolerant views about Armenians. He had personally ensured that his father continue to supply food to the orphanage even after others had refused to do so. But Mariam found it confusing that he paid so much attention to her.

"Thank you for bringing the supplies," she said. And then she hurried out to check on the tonir.

Kevork was still fast asleep in his dormitory at Beitshalom, the boys' orphanage at the other end of the missionary compound. He didn't even begin to waken until the Mairig rang the morning bell. He had tossed and turned most of the night, trying to get to sleep, and then he finally drifted off just as the first rays of dawn lit the room.

He turned his face, then felt the cold dampness of his pillow. In a flash, the sadness of the evening before came back to him.

Kevork was the most senior shoemaking apprentice, and so Mr. Karellian had taken to leaving him alone in the workshop once lessons were over. In addition to a personal project Kevork had been working on, he was responsible for putting away all the supplies and turning off the lights at the end of the day. Kevork enjoyed his hour or so of solitude in the workshop each day, but last night his solitude had been disturbed by a knock on the door.

It was Josefine Younger, looking just a bit greyer around the temples than she had six years earlier when Kevork had arrived. Today, instead of her usual pleasant smile, her brow was creased with worry.

Classes were over, but Kevork had stayed late in order to assist the first-year apprentice with the re-soling of an old shoe. The shoe in question was covering a wooden last, or shoe form, on a stand, and the apprentice had already partially loosened the original lacing with rubbing alcohol.

When Kevork saw Miss Younger's expression, he turned to the boy and said, "You can go now. When you come in tomorrow, start back at this shoe, but be careful with the lacing."

The boy nodded, then scampered out.

Kevork stood up to greet her.

"Please," he said. "Come in." He pulled out a work stool from under the wooden bench and set it in front of her. "Please sit down."

Miss Younger stayed standing. "A letter came for you," she said. "Perhaps you should sit." She reached into her pocket and drew out a yellowed envelope of cheap paper.

Kevork reached out and took it with apprehension. From time to time, others at the orphanage had received letters, too, but he could not remember a single time when a letter bore happy news.

It felt heavier than just paper. He looked at the handwriting and frowned. It wasn't familiar. The back was sealed with red wax. He broke the seal and reached inside.

There was a handful of gold coins and two sheets of paper. He unfolded the first one and read:

Dear Kevork,

I have thought of you often in these last years, and every time I was in your village, I would stop by your old house to see if your father had come back so I could tell him where you were. I found out that he did come back briefly several months ago. He left these gold coins for you in care of the people who now live in your home. They entrusted them to me to give to you.

Apparently, he had been arrested and jailed as a revolutionary by the Turkish government. No sooner did he get back to his home village than he was taken again. This time, he was drafted into the Turkish army.

The enclosed letter arrived at your old house recently, and the people who now live there had it sent to me.

*I am sorry to be the bearer of this bad
news, but I realize that you need to know
the fate of your father.*

*Your friend in Allah,
Abdul Hassan*

Kevork opened the second sheet of paper with
trembling hands. It was an official-looking letter from
the Turkish army. It was dated March 2, 1915, and stated that his father had died of "heart failure" while on
duty. He crumpled the paper up and threw it on the
ground with anger and sadness.

Josefine Younger reached down and picked up the
paper. She folded it smooth and then read for herself.
"Heart failure," she said. "Yet another."

Kevork raised his eyes to hers. "What do you mean?"

"Rumour has it that all the Armenians drafted into
the Turkish army were executed."

"But it says 'heart failure,'" said Kevork.

"As do all the other letters," replied Miss
Younger. "I suppose they're correct. Execution does
cause heart failure."

She set the crumpled letter down on the work-
bench, then stepped over to Kevork. Even though he
was a head taller than she was, she gave him a mother-
ly hug. "I am so sorry for your loss."

Kevork hugged her tightly and swallowed back
his tears.

The bell rang again, jolting Kevork out of his memories. The sun had risen further, and now his dormitory

room was fully visible. Kevork moved his head left and right and saw that he was the only one still in his cot. All of the other boys had dressed and made their beds and were at breakfast. Kevork reached under his pillow and felt the edges of the papers with his fingertips. So it wasn't all just a terrible nightmare: his father really was dead. He reached in further and touched the envelope, in which he'd wrapped the gold coins. He drew the envelope out and dumped the contents onto his palm. Nine gold coins. This was the sum total of his family now.

He closed his palm around the gold and held it to his heart. His father was dead, but Kevork was comforted by the fact that his father had tried to come back to find him. He hadn't been abandoned after all. As he lay there alone in the dormitory room with a fistful of gold resting on his heart, Kevork first said a prayer for the soul of his father, and then he made a pledge. "I will live in a way that would make my father proud."

Then he wiped the remnants of tears from his face and sat up to start a new day.

Aunt Anna's white hair was pulled back into a bun and the sleeves of her white shirt were rolled up above her elbows. She was kneading a huge round of golden dough by the time Mariam walked back into the kitchen.

"I saw Rustem Bey leave just as I was coming in," said Anna.

Anna had aged hardly at all in the last six years. In fact, if anything, she seemed to have gotten younger. The constant frown of worry that lined her face after the Adana massacre had softened, and she had gained some weight, making her pallid skin look healthier.

"I don't know what to make of him," said Mariam. "I'm surprised that his father lets him speak to me so much." Mariam washed her hands, then grabbed an apron from a peg and tied it around her waist.

"In fact," said Anna, giving Mariam a meaningful look, "I wouldn't be surprised if Rustem Bey had his father pay a visit to your grandmother." She gave the round of dough she was working on one last punch on the flour-covered table, then said to Mariam, "This batch is ready to shape."

Mariam looked at Anna in shock. There was only one reason that Rustem's father would pay a visit to her family, and that would be to ask for her hand in marriage. Both Turks and Armenians followed this tradition of arranged marriage.

The two worked side by side in friendly silence, each considering weightier things. They divided the dough into balls, then rolled each ball out flat and thin. The flat circles of dough were doused with flour, then stacked in a mound on a large wooden platter.

"You can't be serious," said Mariam. "Anahid Baji would never make me marry a Turk."

Anna looked up from the dough she was working on and met Mariam's eyes. "Your grandmother would do whatever she felt was in your best interests."

"I can't imagine it would be that," replied Mariam, flushing in anger.

She took a bowl of water then stepped outside to check on the baking pit, glad to get away from Anna and the conversation for the moment. The heat from the pit made her flush even deeper as she stuck her head through the opening of the shed and looked down at the glowing red coals. She dipped her fingers into the water then flicked it onto the hot stone sides. It sizzled in an instant. The baking pit was ready.

She walked back into the kitchen.

Anna looked at her with a flash of frustration in her eyes. "Do you not understand what is happening?" she asked.

"What do you mean?" asked Mariam.

"The Turkish government is rounding up all the Armenians and deporting them. If you married Rustem, you would be safe. And you would be in a position to protect your family."

Mariam's eyes filled with tears. "She wouldn't ask me to do that," she said. "Besides, they are only rounding up the men."

Anna's lips were pressed into a thin line of disapproval, but she said nothing more on the subject. The two worked together in silence for the moment.

Mr. Karellian didn't say a word when Kevork walked into the workshop fifteen minutes late, but instead nodded to him in sympathy and got back to assisting Dikran, the first-year apprentice, in the art of waxing and twisting a sturdy length of linen thread which would then be used to sew on soles.

There were six boys altogether besides Kevork who were in training: one for each year of apprenticeship.

He looked at the row of boys sitting in order of age and size, all working industriously on their various projects. What did the future hold for these boys? wondered Kevork. Best not to think of that too much.

There were two things that Kevork had been working on. One was the project that Mr. Karellian had set for him, and that was to make himself a pair of boots. Most of the orphans wore mismatched sets of cast-off shoes and boots donated from North America and England. And most of what the shoemaking apprentices worked on was re-soling old shoes, matching them into sets as best they could and patching holes. However, Mr. Karellian was an optimist, and he felt that his charges should be prepared for the outside world after the war: perhaps a life in another country. So in addition to the practical work of fixing old shoes, apprentices in their last year were required to make one pair of boots from scratch for themselves. Kevork had been required to skin a dead cow, scrape the hide, tan it, make a custom shoe pattern, then cut the leather to shape.

With Mr. Karellian's permission, Kevork had taken on a second project. Not only was he making himself a pair of boots, but he was also making a pair for Marta. Mr. Karellian's one admonition was that he work on Marta's boots only once all the other apprentices had left. Cowhide was hard to come by, and he didn't want to set a precedent.

Before Kevork took down his own pair of boots to work on, he went over to the corner where Marta's were stored. He lifted up the corner of the oilcloth and took a peek. They were there. And they were almost finished.

By the time Anna and Mariam were finished baking all the bread, morning classes at the orphanage had ended, and the girls at Bethel had an hour of free time before prayer service and lunch.

Mariam wanted to visit Anahid Baji. Was it true what Anna had told her? Was Rustem Bey really going to ask for her hand? Mariam wrapped a few fresh loaves in a square of cloth and then ran out of the kitchen.

As she hurried down the street towards the double gates at the entrance, she passed Paris and a couple of other girls. They were playing hide and seek. Another girl, who must have been new because Mariam didn't recognize her, was sitting on the ground, watching the others with forlorn eyes. The sight brought a lurch to Mariam's heart. She remembered how lonely she'd been when she arrived six years earlier, and she'd had her sister to keep her company. Mariam stopped. She squatted down on her heels so that she was eye-level with the new girl.

"Are you hungry?" Mariam asked in a soft voice. She opened up her square of cloth with the still-warm bread.

The little girl drew her eyes away from the game of hide and seek and looked at Mariam. Her nose wrinkled at the aroma of the bread, and then the pink tip of her tongue darted out and wet her lips. She nodded hesitantly.

Mariam broke off a bite-sized piece and placed it in the girl's palm. The girl looked at it for a moment, then popped it into her mouth. "Thank you," she said.

Mariam held out the rest of one loaf.

The girl's eyes brightened. "Really?"

Mariam nodded, then placed it in her hands. "What's your name?"

"Parantzim," said the girl.

Mariam had a momentary start. Images of her own dead mother came back, but she quickly suppressed them. "You'll be fine here," said Mariam. "Just come to the kitchen if ever you're lonely or hungry."

Parantzim flashed Mariam a brief smile of gratitude, then concentrated on devouring the bread.

Mariam stood back up, then hurried down the street to the orphanage gates. She had to see her grandmother! She reached up to unlatch the door.

"Mariam, stop."

Mariam turned around. Miss Younger's brow was beaded with perspiration and there was a look of concern in her eyes. "You cannot go out onto the street by yourself right now."

"Why not?" asked Mariam. "I have done it before."

"Just yesterday, one of our older girls was accosted in the market. The political unrest is making it unsafe."

"But I have to see my grandmother," said Mariam.

"You cannot go alone," said Miss Younger.

Mariam knew better than to argue. She walked back with Miss Younger towards the central complex of buildings. Marta would be finished her lessons, and Mariam knew where she could be found.

As Miss Younger turned towards her own office in the administrative building, Mariam continued to walk down the main street of the orphanage complex until she reached Beitshalom at the far end.

She passed a group of barefoot boys playing ball in the boys' courtyard, and then passed Mr. Karellian and a few of the German missionaries, who were sitting at a table under the shade of a tree in front of the teachers' sleeping quarters. Mr. Karellian and one of the missionaries were playing a game of chess. The others were watching and sipping steaming cups of Armenian coffee.

Mr. Karellian looked up as she passed and smiled. She inclined her head to him, but didn't stop.

She could see that the door to the shoemaking workshop was wide open even before she got there. This meant that Marta was likely there with Kevork. If Kevork was there by himself, or the workshop was empty, the door would have been closed. The only time the door was left wide open was when Kevork had a female visitor. And that visitor was invariably Marta.

Mariam rapped on the open door. "Come in," called Kevork.

Kevork and Marta were each sitting on work stools facing each other, their knees not touching, but only inches apart. It surprised her to see them like this. She knew that they were fast friends, but today they looked like more than that. She regarded her sister and realized that the childishness she had seen there in the darkness of the morning had been more in her mind than reality. Marta was a young woman. It wasn't just the soft curve in her breast, or the leanness that was beginning to show in her face. More than anything, it was the way she was looking at Kevork.

As Mariam stepped into the room, Marta brushed the corner of her eye with the back of her hand, and Kevork stuffed a piece of paper into his shirt pocket.

"Is there something wrong?" Mariam asked, looking from the one to the other.

Marta stayed silent and looked down at her hands. Kevork reached over to Marta and touched her arm, and then he looked up to Mariam.

"My father is dead," he said.

"My God," said Mariam. "I am so sorry." She walked over to Kevork and Marta and placed her bundle of bread on the worktable. She knelt down where they were sitting and wrapped an arm around each. They stayed like that in silence for several minutes.

Kevork broke the silence. "You came in here looking like you were about to tell us something. Not more sad news, I hope?"

"No," said Mariam. "I wanted to visit Anahid Baji, but Miss Younger warned me not to go alone."

"Because of the unrest?" asked Kevork. "She mentioned to me that the Turks are cracking down on Armenians even more than they were."

"Yes," said Mariam.

"There is something Aunt Anna needs to ask Anahid Baji on my behalf," said Kevork. "Perhaps we should all go together?"

Marta appeared startled and looked up at this last comment, and Mariam caught her eye. There was only one question that Aunt Anna would ask on Kevork's behalf, and that would be a marriage proposal.

It was a sad testament to the times that the question would be asked without parents. Instead of the father of the prospective groom asking the father of the prospective bride, it would be an aunt asking a grandmother.

When they entered the Armenian district, Mariam knew that something was very wrong. There was a stray goat stumbling on the cobblestones, bleating in distress, and there was a faint metallic smell in the air.

"Look," said Marta, pointing down around their feet. Hundreds of chicken feathers speckled with blood were scattered about. The only sound in the air was the howling of wild dogs in the distance.

"Quickly," said Mariam. "We must get to Anahid Baji's."

With hearts pounding, the group ran down the winding street and around the corner to Anahid Baji's house. The latch was broken on the gate and the door creaked eerily in the windless air. A bunch of grapes, mashed with a boot print, stained the entrance.

The scene brought back a rush of terrible memories for Mariam. It was just like Adana. A vivid image of stepping into Kevork's house so many years ago and the horror of Arsho's empty cradle filled her mind. She stepped past the broken gate and ran through the garden that she had known since she was a child. The front door of her grandmother's house was unlocked and it opened with a sigh when she pushed on it.

What struck her first when she stepped inside was the coldness. There was no fire in the ojak. Not even a single ember. The big bed had been put away behind the wall curtains, but the floor was dusty with footprints. In the midst of the footprints was Arsho's little pillow from so many years ago. Mariam picked it up and dusted it off, then sat down on the edge of the hearth, resting the pillow in her lap. Onnig had come to love this pillow. And even as he got older, he had kept it. Had he discarded it now, or had they left so quickly that he dropped it?

The others had stepped in by this time, and Marta climbed the steps to look on the roof while Kevork lifted the carpet from the entrance to the root cellar to check down there. Empty.

Anna walked over to Anahid Baji's hope chest and opened it. Empty.

Anna sat down beside Mariam. She reached out and touched the discarded pillow with her fingertip. "Where could they have gone?" she asked.

"I don't know," said Mariam. And why didn't they tell her first? The only way Anahid Baji and Ovsanna and the children would leave without telling Mariam and Marta would have been under force. The thought sent shivers through her.

When Marta came down from the roof, her face was very pale.

Mariam set the pillow down on the mantle of the ojak and stood up. "What is it?" she asked Marta.

"I could see the strangest thing when I looked in the distance. A huge snake of dust — beyond the walls of Marash. I could make out oxcarts and people walking. Countless people walking towards the desert."

CHAPTER NINE

"Hurry!" cried Miss Younger as they stumbled through the outer gates of the orphanage complex. "I was afraid you would never get back here."

The foursome had managed to convince six urchins from the street to come with them as they rushed through the winding streets back to the orphanage. One little boy had stumbled and fallen, and Kevork had picked him up and carried him most of the way in his arms. Marta had two little girls — each holding one of her hands — and Mariam carried a toddler. Anna carried the younger sister of an eight-year-old boy who followed close by her heels.

Miss Younger pushed them all inside and then locked the gate behind them. Mariam was taken aback by the wild look in her eyes. "The deportations have started," Miss Younger said. "And not just the men."

The statement hit Mariam like a blow. It explained what happened to Anahid Baji, Ovsanna, and the children. And it explained what Marta had seen in the distance. She set the toddler down and clutched onto her sister's shoulder so she wouldn't fall.

"The orphanage has been given notice that all of the Armenian adults on staff will be deported."

"You cannot let that happen," said Mariam.

"I have no choice," replied Miss Younger. "Death is the penalty for hiding an Armenian adult."

"What about the children?" asked Mariam.

"The mayor has assured me that as long as we co-operate with the Turkish army officials tomorrow, the children will not be harmed."

"Thank God," said Mariam.

"However," continued Miss Younger, "we must all assemble in the courtyard tomorrow at dawn, bags packed, and ready for further instruction."

"Even the children?" asked Mariam.

"Yes."

Aunt Anna could see the fear forming in the eyes of the urchins who had followed them into the orphanage complex for safety. "Come with me," she said, pasting a brave smile on her face. "I will get you some hot soup, and then a bath and clean clothing."

As she herded the new children towards the kitchen, she turned her head towards Kevork. "You and Marta and Mariam must prepare for tomorrow. Go."

Miss Younger followed Anna, carrying the toddler. Mariam, Kevork, and Marta were left standing just inside the locked gate.

"What shall we do?" asked Mariam, a look of desperation in her eyes. "Will the Turks consider us children or adults?"

Kevork didn't want to say it out loud, but he was certain that they would all be considered adults. And while his father was killed by the Turkish army, there were worse things that could happen to women.

"If we can stay together, we have more chance of surviving," said Kevork.

"The Turks will separate the sexes," said Mariam. "That is a certainty."

"Then either I must disguise myself as a woman, or you two must dress as boys," said Kevork, "but we must stay together."

Mariam regarded Kevork's height, muscular shoulders, and bristled face. "You would make a singularly unconvincing girl."

Kevork looked from Mariam to Marta and had similar concerns. Marta was tall and solid, and her face was more handsome than pretty. With her hair cut and dressed in men's clothing, she could pass for a tall boy. Mariam was far too delicate. Her narrow fingers would look feminine even if their almond-shaped nails were cut short and smudged with dirt. And her figure. How much would boy's clothing hide? But what else could they do? He swallowed back his doubts.

"We all need to dress as males," said Kevork.

Mariam nodded.

"I will go to the boys' laundry and see what I can find for you," said Kevork.

"Thank you," said Mariam.

"My father left me some money," said Kevork, patting his shirt pocket. "Perhaps these coins will help us bribe our way to safety."

"How much do you have?" asked Mariam.

"Nine gold coins," said Kevork. He drew them out of his pocket and showed them to her.

Mariam picked one up and felt its weight. "You should sew them into your clothing so they won't be stolen." She handed it back to him, then turned to her sister and said, "Come back with me now so we can pack food and supplies."

Marta was about to follow her, but Kevork caught her hand.

"I need to talk to you in private," he said.

They walked side by side to the shoemaker's workshop. When they got inside, he closed and locked the door.

"Sit," said Kevork, indicating one of the work stools.

Marta sat.

Kevork leaned forward and clasped her hands. "You know what Anna was going to ask your grandmother today."

Marta nodded, then looked down at their intertwined hands.

"And I want to do this properly. Our families must agree to our marriage, but right now, we're nobody's children."

Marta looked up at him with tear-filled eyes.

He let go of her hands, then stood up and walked over to an oilcloth-covered bundle on the shelf. He lifted the bundle up and brought it over to where Marta sat.

"This was to be my betrothal gift to you."

Marta looked in wonder from the bundle to Kevork's eyes. "Then I shouldn't open it now."

"Times are different," he said. "You'll need these." And with that, he flipped open the cloth.

Marta's eyes widened with delight when she saw the handmade boots. "They're beautiful!" she said.

Kevork smiled sadly. "I only wish I could have given them to you under happier circumstances."

She reached out her hand and touched one of the boots with her fingertip as if to make sure they were real.

Then she lifted her skirt and stuck out her feet. The boots she wore now were a mismatched set. For over a year, Marta had been wearing a tan-coloured lady's boot from England on her right foot, and a boy's brown boot on her left. Kevork had taken off the original heels from each boot and replaced them with new, more comfortable low heels, but the boots themselves had become not only unbearably tight, but worn. A week ago, the side of the lady's boot had split beyond repair.

Kevork knelt down in front of her and took the split tan boot in his hand. He unlaced it, then pulled. It didn't budge.

"Just a minute," said Marta. She wedged the tip of her brown boot at the base of the heel of the tan boot and pushed while Kevork pulled. It slid off. Marta wiggled her toes. "It feels good to get that off," she said.

The brown boot wasn't quite as tight, plus it was made of firmer leather, so it slipped off with less difficulty. Kevork placed the new black boots in front of Marta and she slipped her feet in. Kevork laced them up.

"Stand up," he said.

Marta stood up. She lifted her skirt up again and peered down at them with a sad smile. She walked over to Kevork and wrapped her arms around his neck. "Thank you," she said, then kissed him on the cheek.

Kevork wrapped one arm around her waist, and with the other, he gently placed her head on his shoulder. "I will protect you," he said fiercely.

As Mariam walked to the long, low building that housed her dormitory room, she saw Mr. Karellian leading an empty ox and cart.

As she passed him, she noticed the look of fear in his eyes. "Is that for tomorrow?" she asked him.

"Yes," he said. "It is the only cart we have. I must fill it with all the food and supplies it will carry."

"Where will they be deporting us to?" she asked.

Mr. Karellian's eyes filled with tears. "Beyond the desert," he said. "That is all I know."

The warmth of the sun streaming in through the window woke Mariam up with a start the next morning. Her heart fluttered as she bolted to a sitting position. The room was too silent and still. She looked around and saw that she and Marta were the only ones left in the dormitory. Of all the days to sleep in, this wasn't it. She threw off the bedcovers and stood up. On top of her chest lay a set of boy's clothing: a coarse linen shirt smelling of soap and a pair of loose trousers. Mariam couldn't even remember Marta coming in the night before and didn't remember her bringing the boys' clothing. Instead of putting them on, she set them aside and drew out her own skirt and blouse.

Once she was dressed, she tucked her mother's sickle into the back of her skirt.

She walked over to Marta's bed and gazed at her sister's untroubled face. What she would give to preserve her sister's happy innocence. If only there was some place they could hide — some way to avert their fate — but she knew that could not be. Better to face it. She gently shook Marta's shoulder. "Marta!" she said. "Wake up."

Marta slept.

Mariam walked over to the dressing table at the far end of the room and picked up the earthen jug. There wasn't much water left in it. Mariam carried the jug over to her sister's bed and splashed the water into her face. Marta sat up with a jolt.

"What did you do that for?" Marta asked, shaking droplets of water from her hair.

"You cannot sleep any longer," said Mariam urgently.

As Marta's covers fell off her, Mariam was surprised to see that she was already wearing a boy's shirt and trousers. Holding up Marta's trousers was a belt made of tiny scraps leather painstakingly hand-stitched together. A gift from Kevork, no doubt.

"When did you change?" she asked.

"Last night, before I went to bed," said Marta, pulling the covers back and getting out of bed. She quickly rolled her bedding into a bundle, then drew her new boots from under the bed.

Mariam looked at the sturdy new boots in wonder. They were identical to the ones that Kevork had been making for himself. She knew instantly that Kevork had wanted to give these to Marta as his betrothal gift. She swallowed back a sob as she thought of how circumstances had changed in the last twenty-four hours. But one thing she knew for sure: Marta was in good hands with Kevork. He would never let anything happen to her.

"Hurry," said Mariam in a brusque voice to hide her tears.

She stood and watched while Marta quickly laced up her boots, and then they grabbed their bedrolls and walked out the door. They ran through the courtyard and back to Beitshalom to find Kevork.

They found him in his room, reading his father's letter one last time as he held the gold coins to his heart. Like Marta, he was dressed in a coarse linen shirt, trousers held up with a leather belt, and sturdy new black boots on his feet.

He looked up when they came in, set the coins and letter on the bed, then drew out a pair of scissors from his shirt pocket. "Sit here, Marta," he said, patting a space beside him on the bed. "It's time to cut your hair."

Mariam watched as hunks of Marta's long hair fell to the floor. To her surprise, with the hair cut short, her sister could pass for a young boy without too much difficulty. Her shoulders relaxed just a bit. Perhaps their plan would work.

"You're next," said Kevork, looking at Mariam.

"No," said Mariam.

"But we agreed," said Kevork.

"I'll take my chances as a girl," she replied. She hoped that Kevork and Marta thought she was simply vain. The last thing she wanted was heroics on their part. She knew that she would never successfully pass herself off as a boy, and she was afraid that if she tried, the Turks would twig onto her sister's disguise.

"Your coins, Kevork," she said, changing the subject. "You haven't sewn them into your clothing."

"I decided that we should each take three," he replied. "That way, if we're separated, we'll each still have something to live on."

A sob caught in Mariam's throat. Kevork's generosity was overwhelming. Mariam took the first three coins and held them reverently in her palm. These coins could be the difference between life and death.

Kevork had a spool of thread and a needle ready. "Turn around," Mariam said to him. "I want to open up the seam in your collar and hide one there." With the scissors that had recently made her sister look like a boy, Mariam carefully opened up the seam on the underside of Kevork's collar and tucked in one coin, then stitched it back together. She hid another one in the cuff of his shirt, and another in the waistband of his trousers. She did the same for Marta.

When she lifted up her own skirt to sew a coin into her seam, the sickle dislodged and fell to the ground. Marta reached down and picked it up.

"Are you taking this?" asked Marta, running her finger along the sharp edge.

"Don't," said Mariam, grabbing the sickle. "You'll hurt yourself." She tucked it back into the waist of her skirt, then said, "Are we ready?"

"We'd better be," said Kevork. "The assembly is being inspected in mere minutes."

The three grabbed their bedrolls and ran out.

They were among the last to assemble in the courtyard.

Most of the two hundred orphans were quite young, and they were sitting in neat rows on the ground, using their bedrolls as cushions. Mariam was struck by the fact that she had never witnessed such silence in these children before. Two hundred pairs of eyes followed Mariam, Marta, and Kevork as they took their places in the front row. Directly behind Mariam sat Paris, the little girl who had first greeted them six years ago. Mariam turned and gave her an encouraging smile.

Anna, Miss Younger, Mr. Karellian, and the other missionaries and teachers stood to one side.

Just then, the gates were thrown open, and a Turkish officer on a white stallion entered in a swirl of dust, followed by soldiers on foot. While the soldiers were dressed in coarse uniforms of dull brown, the officer was smartly dressed in a dark blue uniform with a stiffly starched red upright collar and matching red cuffs, knee-length black leather boots, a black leather belt holding a bayonet and a pistol, and a tall tasselled red fez on his head.

Mariam knew who he was by reputation alone: Mahmoud Sayyid, captain of the Turkish army in Marash. The sight of his handsome, mustached face and signature white horse instilled fear wherever he went. There were stifled whimpers from the children sitting behind Mariam.

His eyes looked cruel, but the skin on his face and hands were soft and pampered. His uniform was clean and crisp, and even his boots, although covered with a fine mist of dust, looked barely walked in. Mariam could imagine him standing in front of a mirror and preening like a woman.

Captain Sayyid dismounted and handed his reins to one of the soldiers. First, he approached the group of adults. "Where are the Armenians?" he said.

Anna stepped forward. So did Mr. Karellian. The laundress, Tante Maria, also hesitantly stepped forward, as did the two other Armenian teachers.

"Where are you hiding the rest?" asked Captain Sayyid, staring fiercely at Miss Younger.

"These are all," she said.

"You lie," he said.

Then he turned to face the rows of trembling children. "Stand," he ordered.

The children all stood, clutching bedrolls to their chests.

With his hands clasped behind his back, Captain Sayyid walked to the end of the first row, then strutted forward between the rows of frightened children, stopping now and again for a second look. When he got to the front of the row, he found Kevork and stopped.

Kevork tried to minimize his height by keeping his knees bent, but even so, he was a head taller than the Captain.

He turned to Miss Younger. "This is no child."

"He is merely fifteen," said Miss Younger.

"I don't believe you." With a motion of his hand, he ordered Kevork to join the adults.

Next, he stepped in front of Marta. Like Kevork, she was consigned to the adult group.

Mariam's heart beat wildly as he stopped in front of her. She held her bedroll to her chest and tried to relax her face into childlike innocence. She and the Captain were nose to nose in height. He leaned in so close to her face that she could smell the sickly sweet pomade in his hair. A smile formed on his lips. He reached out his hand and gently brushed her cheek. She cringed.

"Where have you been hiding this one?" he asked Miss Younger.

Mariam reached one hand behind her, and, unobtrusively as she could, she felt the outline of the sickle through her skirt.

"You will come with me," he said.

"I will not go," she said firmly. She slipped a finger through the belt of her skirt and worked the handle of the sickle loose.

With a cold smile, he drew out his pistol. Mariam held her breath. Perhaps this was the best way to go. To be killed now and have it end. But he pointed the gun directly behind her and shot.

Mariam felt something warm and wet on the handle of her sickle. She turned, then screamed. Blood.

Paris. Dear Paris. The little girl had been shot. Her neck gurgled with blood and she gasped, trying to get a breath of air. She fell into the arms of the girl standing behind her.

Captain Sayyid pointed his pistol towards the adults. "No one move, or you will be next."

Mariam watched him with tear-filled anger as he decided the fates of the rest of the children. Some who were as young as ten were assigned to the "adult" group and set for deportation.

When he was finished, he grabbed Mariam's hand and pulled her towards his horse. He lifted her as if she were no more than a doll and pushed her onto his saddle. Then he put his boot in the stirrup and nearly kicked her as he got on the horse in front of her.

Mariam leaned back on her hands to avoid his boot, and as she did so, her one bloodied hand branded the horse's rump. The sickle slipped out of her skirt. She tried to grab it, but she was too late. All she saw was a flicker of metal disappearing in a swirl of dust.

As the stallion galloped through the gates, she was forced to hold the Captain's belt so she wouldn't fall off. Unaware of the last bit of blood that had smeared on his clean uniform, he smiled approvingly at her. "That's more like it," he said.

She turned her head. The last thing she saw was her sister and Kevork and the other "adults" herded together by soldiers with bayonets. Their desperate plan had not worked at all. All three of them had been deemed "adults" and they had been split apart. Her one comfort was knowing that Marta had successfully hidden her gender and that she and Kevork would — for the moment — be together.

CHAPTER TEN

Mariam felt nauseous when she looked down and saw the ground moving under her. She tightened her grip on the officer's belt, but felt a wave of bile rise in her throat. The smell of his pomade mixed with sweat was overpowering. For a brief moment Mariam considered loosening her grip from the officer's belt and falling off the horse, but then she looked around she saw that the Marash she knew no longer existed. As the stallion travelled down a street in the Turkish district, Mariam saw that the houses were shut tight. There were no children playing in the streets or housewives gossiping behind courtyard gates. Even the roofs were empty. Once, Mariam saw a veiled women's eyes peeking out at her through a latticed window. After that, Mariam had a vague sense of being watched.

When they left the Turkish district and entered the Armenian section, things changed again. It was silent and still as it had been in the other parts of the city, but here the silence was from emptiness rather than hiding. While in the Turkish district, the only smell that Mariam had been aware of was that of the officer's sweat and hair, but now there was another odour. One that lingered on the tip of her memory. Faintly metallic. Faintly rotting.

The stallion came to a dead stop. Mariam craned her neck to see over the officer's shoulder. The road was blocked by an oxcart loaded to overflowing with household goods. A chandelier, bolts of rich cloth, a large intricately carved wooden wardrobe, kitchen pots.

What confused her was that the man holding the reins of the oxcart wore an ill-fitting Turkish army uniform, but he didn't look like a soldier.

"Move aside," said Captain Sayyid firmly.

The man whipped the ox and its bellow echoed in the eerie silence, and it took a few steps forward, clearing a space in the road just wide enough for the officer's horse to step through. As they passed, the man grinned lewdly at Mariam, revealing rotted teeth. He turned to Captain Sayyid and said, "I see I'm not the only one gathering up Armenian riches."

Mariam trembled.

The stallion got just a few houses further down the narrow winding street before there was another obstruction. This time, it was a small pyramid of household goods abandoned in the middle of the road. There was bedding, a half-empty sack of grain, worn and patched clothing. Whoever had plundered it wasn't satisfied with the meagreness of his loot.

As Captain Sayyid manoeuvred the horse around it, Mariam couldn't help but visualize the terrorized family who had been ordered out of their home and then robbed of these poor items. Where was that family now?

They continued down the street, through scenes of abandonment and plunder, until they arrived at a stately home in the oldest part of the Armenian district. Mariam knew that this house belonged to Hagop Topalian, a wealthy Armenian jeweller. Hagop's brother had been the mayor of Marash before the Young Turks overthrew the Sultan, but the family's influence had diminished in the last years.

The Captain dismounted and tethered the horse to the gate.

Mariam slid off the horse, stumbling and landing on her hands and knees in the litter-strewn street.

He prodded her with the toe of his boot. "Get up," he said.

She stumbled to her feet and he pushed her towards the open gate in the street wall. Mariam was overcome with fear, but she willed herself not to show it. She decided that she had to concentrate on memorizing every detail of everything that she passed. Perhaps this information would somehow help her escape.

Forcing herself to concentrate, she noticed that the exterior of the huge house looked dull and weathered, but Mariam saw that the walkway through the garden was a beautiful mosaic in subtle tones of white, grey, and wheat-coloured marble. The garden itself was abundant with flowering shrubs and fragrant lemon trees, but some of the trees had been bent to the ground, and one was snapped in half. There were bits of debris on the walkway — broken china, shards of crystal, stains. And muddied footsteps.

There were three white marble steps that led to a wide double door of intricately carved wood. The doors were weathered and dark, but beautiful nonetheless. The Captain held the door open and pushed Mariam inside. Mariam noted that the door was not locked.

CHAPTER ELEVEN

Kevork stared down the barrel of the gun that was pointed at his nose.

"Tomorrow morning at dawn," said the soldier, "you will all gather back here for deportation."

Kevork nodded. The soldier lowered his weapon. "Any Armenian who resists deportation will be shot," said the soldier. "And any Turk who assists an Armenian will have his house burned to the ground, then he will have to watch while that 'saved' Armenian is executed."

With that, the soldier turned and left. The others who had aimed their weapons at Marta, Anna, and the rest of their group lowered them. They followed the first soldier out the gate.

As soon as they were gone, Miss Younger ran to Paris. Mara, the girl who had caught her, was slick with blood. She had stumbled to the ground with the weight of Paris.

Miss Younger knelt, then gathered Paris in her arms. As she ran to the orphanage hospital, Kevork could hear her pleading voice, "Please God, let her live."

He felt the warmth of Marta's hand in his. "I must go," she said. She let go of his hand and followed Miss Younger.

The children dispersed in silence. Some followed Miss Younger and Marta. Others walked towards their dormitory rooms.

Kevork lingered, walking over to where the stallion had stood. With the toe of one newly made boot, he traced the hoof marks in the dust. Anna lingered too. She walked up to Kevork. "Nephew," she said, "I know that this is hard for you. It is hard for me, too, but we will pull through. Trust in God."

Kevork looked up at her with a flash of anger. "God?" he said. "If there was a God, he wouldn't let this happen."

Anna's hand flew to her mouth and she regarded Kevork with sorrow. "Even in the darkest times, God gives us people to love," she said. She stood on her toes and kissed him quickly on the cheek and then she turned and walked away.

Kevork was left alone in the courtyard. He stared at the orphanage gates and thought of poor Mariam, carried off by a Turk. He thought of his mother. Was she still alive? What was her fate? Would Mariam's be the same?

He looked down at the pattern his boot was making in the dirt and he noticed something flickering in the sunlight. He knelt down in the dirt and felt with his hands. Mariam's sickle. She must have dropped it.

Kevork picked it up. It was coated with a light layer of dirt. He cleaned it with the sleeve of his shirt, then held it in both hands, feeling its weight. "Bad luck," he said to himself. "Wherever this sickle goes, it causes bad luck."

He knew that Marta would want to preserve it. The sickle was her only memento of her mother, after all. But Kevork was loath to let her have it. He took it with him back to his workshop and hid it in the corner of the very top shelf.

Marta met him as he was locking the door to the workshop. "Paris has died," she said, with tears in her eyes.

"Perhaps she's the lucky one," replied Kevork.

CHAPTER TWELVE

The room that Mariam stepped into was spacious, almost cavernous. The floor was of pale yellow marble, and by the fade marks, it was obvious that a huge carpet had recently covered most of it. Similarly, the plain white plaster walls were bare, but there were hooks along the upper edge. The rich silk wall hangings and paintings that had recently adorned the room had been taken down. In front of a massive marble fireplace, a desk had been set up, and sitting behind it was a man in a loose cotton robe and a tasselled fez, holding a quill pen and frowning over lists on paper.

The man looked up when the Captain pushed Mariam forward. "Is this one for you, or is she for sale?" the man asked in a businesslike voice.

"Let's see what price she will fetch," said the Captain.

The man dipped his pen into ink and then wrote something on the paper in front of him. Without looking up, he said, "Name."

"Give him your name," said Captain Sayyid.

"Mariam."

"Age?"

"Sixteen."

"Are you whole?" asked the man.

"Wh-what do you mean?" asked Mariam.

"Deformities," stated the Captain. "Do you have scars? Have you broken bones?"

"No," said Mariam.

"Disrobe," said the man at the desk in a bored voice.

"What?" asked Mariam.

"Take off your clothing," said the Captain, frowning with cold impatience.

"I won't," she said. No man had ever seen her naked.

The Captain punched her in the stomach so hard that it took her breath away. She fell, sprawling on the floor. He dusted off his hands. "There are many ways of hurting you without it showing."

Mariam looked up at him with unadulterated hatred. She stumbled back to her feet. Spasms of pain coursed through her abdomen, but she willed herself not to cry.

"Do as the man asked," he said.

With trembling fingers and a bright red face, Mariam complied.

"Turn around," said the man at the desk.

Mariam did. She kept her eyes lowered, but she could feel the clerk's and Captain's gazes burning into her flesh.

"Good," he said. "You can get dressed."

As Mariam fumbled back into her clothing with hot tears of anger burning her cheeks, she heard the man say to the Captain, "You've found yourself quite a prize. She'll fetch a good price."

"Yes," said the Captain. "Just remember that it was me who brought her in."

The man looked up from his list. "Of course," he said, with a toothless smile. Then he picked up a bell from the desk and rang it twice.

Without another word, the Captain turned and left. Mariam stood there, alone with the clerk and her anger. She willed herself to look passive. Anger would get her nowhere right now. A few moments passed, then a door opened. A short Turkish woman bent with age and covered from head to foot in a black chador entered the room. The only part of her face that showed were her eyes, and they were wrinkled and rheumy. The woman extended a gnarled hand and grasped Mariam by the elbow. "Come with me," she said, not unkindly.

When Mariam stepped forward, her knees buckled beneath her. She didn't know if it was from the pain in her abdomen, the shock of the situation, or the worry she had for all her loved ones. What was happening with Marta, Kevork, and Anna? What about Anahid Baji, Ovsanna, and the children?

The woman put a firm arm around Mariam's waist to support her, then led her back through the door and down a long hallway. Mariam's breath came in gulps as she tried to deal with the pain and keep her composure. She willed herself to take note of everything she passed. It could mean the difference between life and death.

There were two doors on one side of the hallway and one double door on the other side. All three doors were closed, and in each doorknob was a key. As in the main room, valuable goods had obviously been stolen from the hallway. There were unfaded squares on the walls where pictures had recently hung, and there was a bare wooden table at the far end of the hallway. The floor itself was bare pale hardwood, with darker strips of hardwood closer to the walls. The long runner carpet that had graced the hallway had obviously been pilfered.

The woman stopped in front of the double doors and turned the key, then pulled the door open. "In, please," she said to Mariam, guiding her by the elbow and leading her in.

The air in the room was humid with sweat, and Mariam had trouble seeing because there was a heavy curtain on the window and no lights in the room. She stepped forward. The old woman stepped back out into the hallway. The door closed and there was a loud click as the key turned in the lock.

"Sit here," said a woman's voice from somewhere on the floor. Mariam knelt down, then felt around her with her hands. She could feel sleeping pillows scattered on top of a woven carpet. As her eyes adjusted to the darkness, she could also make out the form of a woman lying on her side on one of the pillows.

"May I pull back the curtain?" asked Mariam.

"If you wish," said the voice.

Mariam stayed on her hands and knees and felt her way towards the window. She reached out and felt the texture of heavy silk brocade. She drew it sideways. Light streamed into the room from outside, bringing with it a gust of cool breeze. Squinting from the sudden light,

Mariam felt around the window frame, then found a tasseled sash and tied the curtain back.

She looked outside and gasped. In better times, the window had looked out onto a carefully tended garden at the back of the house. Spring flowers and fruit trees were in full bloom. There was a beautiful man-made pond surrounded by flagstones, and a fountain in the shape of a dolphin, water streaming from its mouth and cascading into the pond.

It should have been an idyllic scene. But the pond was congested with three bloated, rotting corpses of men. Over the fragrance of fruit trees and flowers, there was the scent of death.

She turned to look inside the room. Next to the woman who had spoken to her, there was a girl of no more than twelve. She was a delicate beauty with cascades of hair so black it was almost blue. Her face was white with sorrow. She sat with her knees clutched up to her chin. Now that there was light in the room, she could see that the other woman was older — perhaps in her thirties. There was a resemblance between the two, and Mariam deduced that they were perhaps mother and daughter. The mother was injured. She wore a simple grey skirt and blouse, but there was a mottled stain of blood on the front of the skirt. There was also a thin dried slash of blood on the side of her face. The woman breathed shallowly, as if in pain.

It was too much for Mariam to take in all at once. She crumpled into a heap on one of the pillows and burst into tears.

The girl crawled over to Mariam and wrapped her arms around her. "It is all right," she said. And then she dissolved into tears, too.

A rush of memories came back to Mariam. Being comforted by her mother so many years ago, Anahid Baji's strong comforting arms. She felt so badly for this little girl, and guilty that she had let herself be seen as so weak that she had to be comforted by a child.

Mariam took a deep breath. "I'll be strong," she said. And then she introduced herself.

"My name is Ani," said the girl. She crawled over to the injured woman lying on the pillow and put her hand lightly on the woman's shoulder.

"This is my mother, Herminé Topalian," she said.

Mariam's hand flew to her mouth. "Topalian?" she said. "So this is your house."

"Yes," replied Ani. "And those bodies in the garden are my brother, father, and uncle."

Miss Younger watched with her mouth set in a thin line as the nurse washed Paris's body, then covered her with a shroud. "This cannot go on," she said, more to herself than anyone else.

She stepped out of the front door of the hospital and the midday heat enveloped her like a furnace. Where did the Turks think they were deporting these people to? She had seen them marching in the southeast, seemingly into the desert. It was April now, and the sun was already hot. What would it be like in a month or two months from now?

With these thoughts on her mind, Miss Younger walked with determination down the main road of the orphanage complex in search of Mr. Muller, one of the other German missionaries. She found him in the kitchen with Mr. Karellian, parcelling up bundles of food.

"I need to talk to you," she said to him.

Both Mr. Muller and Mr. Karellian looked up from their work. Mr. Muller set the bundle he was assembling down on the table and stepped outside with her.

"I cannot go out in the city alone," Miss Younger said, with agitation in her voice. "I need you to accompany me."

"Where is it that you want to go?" asked Mr. Muller.

"I must speak to the German consulate," said Miss Younger. "There must be something we can do to stop these deportations."

"I will go with you if you wish," said Mr. Muller, "but it will do no good."

"Why do you say that?" asked Miss Younger.

"Our government is fully aware of the Armenian situation," said Mr. Muller sadly. "In fact, I have heard that the German government has even provided assistance to the Turks in the form of weapons and manpower."

"That is absurd," said Miss Younger heatedly. "Here you and I are: German citizens, helping these Armenians who are being persecuted by the Turkish government, and you're telling me that our government is helping the Young Turks in the persecution?"

Mr. Muller shifted on his feet. "Not exactly," he said.

"Then what do you mean?"

"Germany and Turkey are on the same side in this Great World War that has just recently started."

"I know that," said Miss Younger.

"The weapons and militia they have sent is for the war effort, but it is also being used against the Armenians."

"I must talk to our consulate," said Miss Younger. "They must stop."

"I would suggest that you do not," said Mr. Muller.

"Why?"

"I would be afraid that if you cause too much fuss, we will be ordered home. And then what would happen to these children?"

Miss Younger was silent for a moment. She had not considered that point. "Then what can we do?" she asked, tears of frustration forming in her eyes.

"We can only carry on as best we can," responded Mr. Muller sadly. "I wish there was more that we could do."

"Perhaps your course is the best one for the moment," said Miss Younger. "Continue packing up food parcels."

"I shall," he said. Then turned and walked back into the kitchen.

Miss Younger held back tears of frustration as she walked back to her own office. She had to think this through and determine what she could do without causing more harm.

She sat down at her desk and drew out a blank sheet of paper. She dipped a pen into ink and then stared at the sheet, willing herself to come up with some sort of plan.

A sharp knock sounded on the door. She looked up, startled, and called, "Come in."

Rustem Bey opened the door and stepped in.

"Please," said Miss Younger, surprised, "sit down." She set down her pen and motioned with her hand towards the one chair in front of her desk.

Rustem Bey sat on the edge of the chair and placed his hands on his knees. He looked at the blank piece of paper in front of her and said, "I hope I am not disturbing you."

"It is fine, Rustem," she replied in a tired voice. "What can I do for you?"

"Would you share with me what is happening to the orphans here in light of the newest measures against the Armenians?"

Miss Younger sighed. "I appreciate your concern, Rustem. You have always been a good friend to me and the other missionaries. We have been given assurances that the children will not be harmed."

Rustem Bey breathed a sigh of relief and leaned back on the chair. "Thank God," he said. "I had been told different."

"What had you been told?" asked Miss Younger.

"My mother told me that the deportations were happening even within the orphanage."

"She is partly right," replied Miss Younger, meeting his eyes. "The older orphans have been deemed 'adults' and they're set for deportation. Also, the Armenian trade teachers and staff will all be deported."

"My God," said Rustem Bey. "Are the Young Turks mad?"

"It seems to me that the whole world has gone mad."

"I want to help you," said Rustem. "I can hide some people in my warehouse."

"I cannot let you do that," said Miss Younger. "If you are caught, the Armenians you hid will be executed before your eyes, you will be killed, and your house and warehouse will be burned. Not only can I not let you risk that for your own sake, but for ours, too. Remember, you are my only secure source of food for the orphans."

Rustem Bey stood up and planted his hands on Miss Younger's desk. "I cannot stand by and watch while these people are being deported," he said.

Miss Younger knew exactly how he felt. Hadn't she just said something similar to Mr. Muller?

"Let us bide our time," she said. "There will be opportunity for you to help, but not right now."

Rustem regarded her with frustration. He removed his hands from her desk and sat back down in the chair. He was silent in his thoughts, as was Miss Younger.

"When will the soldiers be back?" he asked.

"Tomorrow at dawn," she said.

"I need to see Mariam," he said.

Miss Younger looked at the man in front of her. So he didn't know. She wished she didn't have to be the one to tell him. "She is not here."

"What do you mean?" asked Rustem Bey, frowning.

Miss Younger sighed, then held her head in her hands. "Captain Mahmoud Sayyid took her with him this morning."

"Say you are jesting."

"I wish I were," said Miss Younger.

"Do you know the business he is in?" he asked.

"I can only guess," she said.

Without saying another word, Rustem Bey got up from the chair and left, slamming the door behind him.

CHAPTER THIRTEEN

Mariam sat up with a start. There was the sound of a key in the door. It was thrown open wide, and the elderly woman in the chador stood there, a basin of water in her hands and a towel draped over her arm.

"Clean yourselves," said the woman. "You will be wanted downstairs shortly."

Wanted downstairs for what? wondered Mariam. She didn't even want to think of the possibilities.

"This woman is injured," said Mariam. "She needs medical attention."

The elderly woman's eyes flickered with concern above the yashmak. She placed the basin of water on the floor just inside the room and handed the towel to Mariam. The old woman's eyes were drawn to the thin line of blood on Herminé's face, and then to her skirt. She frowned.

"This will come to no good," she said, shaking her head in disapproval. "I wish there was something I could do to help."

Mariam looked at the woman's eyes and saw the sincerity. "Thank you," she said.

Mariam's legs were stiff from lying on the cushions, and her abdomen still hurt from the Captain's punch. She didn't see any advantage to making herself look better for whoever would be waiting for them down below. In fact, Mariam surmised, it might be better to look worse. She was more concerned about Herminé's health than anyone's appearance. Mariam dragged the towel and basin of water close to Herminé's cushion.

"Does your face hurt?" asked Mariam.

"No," the woman replied. "But I feel very weak."

Mariam dipped a corner of the towel into the water, then blotted the woman's wound. The dry blood came off, revealing a razor-thin slice underneath. When a thin line of fresh blood seeped through the newly cleaned spot, Mariam decided that she would be better off to leave the dry blood alone so that the wound wouldn't open up again.

Mariam looked at the woman's skirt and noticed that the splotch of blood seemed very fresh.

"Can I help you remove your skirt?" asked Mariam.

Herminé nodded.

Mariam reached behind the woman's skirt and loosened it.

"Let me help," said Ani, frowning in concern at her mother.

Ani sat down on a cushion behind her mother. "Lean on me," she whispered into her mother's ear.

Herminé propped herself up from the cushion she was lying on, then leaned heavily into her daughter's lap. Mariam was able to loosen the skirt and pull it completely off.

Herminé wore beautifully embroidered white lace petticoats beneath, covering her from waist to knee. The petticoats were ripped and glistening with fresh blood.

"God have mercy," cried Mariam. She ripped away the petticoat and tried to staunch the blood, but it was impossible. Mariam looked up into Herminé's eyes and saw that they were glassy. She looked beyond her and into Ani's eyes, which were round with fear.

Herminé's shallow breaths were faint. "Promise me," she whispered hoarsely to Mariam. "Promise me that you'll look after Ani." The effort to say these words was almost more than Herminé could give. She closed her eyes from the effort and relaxed into her daughter's arms. Soon, her breathing became more regular.

Ani placed one hand on her mother's forehead. "She's very cold."

"We must make her comfortable," said Mariam. She shook out the woman's blood-soaked skirt, then gently tucked it around her waist like a blanket.

Ani snuggled into her mother and wrapped her arms around her, trying to warm her. "Are you going to be all right, Mairig?" she asked.

"Yes, love," said Herminé. "I am just going to take a little nap right now."

Ani stayed, holding her mother. Herminé's breathing became shallower with each breath drawn, and then stopped altogether.

As Mariam watched, she sensed that Ani knew intuitively when her mother had died. She watched the young girl squeeze her eyes tight as if to hold in the tears. Then she opened them and looked sadly at Mariam. "Her spirit is at rest now," she said. "She is with my father, brother, and uncle."

At that moment, the key in the handle sounded again and the door opened. Mariam expected to see the old woman. But instead it was a man smelling of liquor. He wore a Turkish army jacket and carried a gun, but his trousers were not army issue. They were cheap and filthy, covered with blood and dirt stains.

He quickly took in the scene and surmised that Herminé was either dead or almost. "Get up," he said, pointing his gun first at Mariam, then at Ani.

Mariam stumbled to her feet, but Ani stayed where she was, gazing defiantly at the man. Mariam reached over to her and tugged her hand. "Come with me," she said. "I told your mother I would look after you." Mariam had no idea how she was going to look after Ani. All she could think of was to keep the girl alive one minute at a time. She couldn't plan further than that.

Ani gently pushed her mother's body forward just a bit so that she could get up. As the girl stood, Mariam saw that her mother's blood had seeped onto the girl's skirt and arms. Ani followed Mariam's gaze, then looked back into her eyes. "I am not washing it off," she said. "This is all I have left of my mother."

Indeed, thought Mariam grimly. And she wasn't about to suggest Ani wash it off. Perhaps the sight of blood would jolt sense into whoever was waiting for them down below.

It was simply a matter of asking the right questions in the right places for Rustem Bey to determine the most likely place to find Mariam. Captain Mahmoud Sayyid's reputation was well known, and many men anticipated this latest sale. Rustem just hoped that he wasn't too late.

It frustrated him to have to backtrack all the way home to fill a purse with gold, but Rustem Bey knew there was no point in travelling to the former Topalian mansion without money — white slave traders didn't deal in handshakes.

When he got to the Topalian mansion, he saw that he was not the first to arrive. There was a cluster of manservants standing just outside the street gate, talking in low voices and smoking cigarettes. As Rustem Bey strode past them with determination, he heard one of the servants chuckle, and then heard his name mentioned. "I didn't think he was one who had to buy his women," a voice said.

He walked through the garden and up the steps and pushed open the heavy wooden double doors. The cavernous room that was devoid of carpets, paintings, and art treasures was now filled with men. Rustem was shocked to see prominent members of Turkish society conversing in bored clusters. He noticed that quite a few regarded his appearance with equal surprise. Amidst the wealthy Turks, there were two farmers, probably looking to buy cheap slaves as field hands. There was also one sun-darkened man in a *thwab* — a loose flowing robe in off-white. On his head was a *guttrah* — a large square of cloth worn on

the head for sun protection. It was held in place with a cir-
clet of black goat's hair and sheep's wool. In spite of his
simple Arabic dress, Rustem recognized the man as Jamal
Aman, whose fabulous wealth was earned by choosing
women for the odalisque market in Smyrna.

A door opened at the far end of the room and a figure dressed in black stepped through. She was followed
by a procession of twenty or so women. In spite of
the fact that they were dishevelled and bloodstained,
Rustem could see that they had been chosen for their
looks. The two farmers noticed this too, and they both
headed for the door.

Rustem pushed his way to the front of the crowd to
get a better look. Many of the "women" were not much
more than children, their eyes round with apprehension. Rustem searched each face. If he could, he would
save them all. He felt the gold coins in his purse and
sighed. Would it even be enough for one?

He craned his neck, looking for Mariam, but she
wasn't there.

Just then a door opened, and a ruffian in half a
Turkish army uniform stepped through. He had two
women by the elbow, and Rustem Bey's jaw dropped. He
recognized them both. There was Mariam! She was bent
slightly over as if in pain, but she did not seem to be too
terribly injured. And there was little Ani Topalian.
Rustem's family and the Topalian family had known each
other for generations. When word got out that the
Topalian mansion had been ransacked, Rustem had
feared the worst for the Topalian brothers, but he had
thought that Herminé and her children, Ani and Hagop

Junior, were safe. He knew they had been visiting relatives in Canada, but he'd had no idea they had come back to Turkey. He gazed at the blood on the little girl's dress and shuddered to think of what it might mean.

He felt the weight of the gold coins in his purse and prayed to Allah.

The clerk sitting at the desk had stood up and was walking over to where the women were lined up. He had a sheaf of paper in his hand. He called names out one by one, and as he did, the girls stepped forward.

"Mari!" he said.

A girl in her mid-teens with a torn dress and hair that looked like it had been hacked short with a knife stepped forward.

"Who will start the bidding?" said the clerk.

"One lira," yelled out a servant hopefully.

"Six," said one of the merchants.

"Eight," said Jamal Aman, the white slave trader from Smyrna.

"Eight lira," said the clerk. "Do I have ten?"
Silence.

"Sold to Jamal Aman for eight Turkish lira."

At the announcement, Mari screamed, then collapsed on the floor. Jamal Aman motioned to his manservant, who was watching the proceedings from the door. The servant walked up to the front and gathered the girl up into his arms, taking her outside. Jamal Aman counted out his eight coins and handed them to the clerk.

Rustem Bey was sickened by the proceeding. To think that a human being could be sold for less than what a bolt of cheap cloth might cost.

The clerk called the next girl, and the next. Like the first, they were both purchased by Jamal Aman. Rustem Bey speculated that the actions against Armenians hadn't started yet in Smyrna. Otherwise, Jamal Aman wouldn't have been so eager to buy so many.

The others in the room were obviously feeling that there would be a glut on the market of girls, and so there was no need to spend too much right now. Rustem had mixed feelings about this. It meant that he would almost certainly have enough to buy both Ani and Mariam, but it also meant that the girls who were being purchased would be forced on a long and uncomfortable journey through desert heat. He shook his head at his thoughts. What was he thinking? If the deportations weren't happening in Smyrna, there was a chance that these girls might live. It was a grim situation all around, but he tried to rationalize with himself that at least these girls might be better off than the other Armenians of Marash. What he tried not to think about was whether they might actually prefer to be dead.

"Ani!" said the clerk.

As Ani Topalian stepped forward, Rustem cursed under his breath. How could he bid on Ani first? What if he ran out of money for Mariam? He drew out his purse, then opened it and quickly did a count. The most any girl had sold for so far had been forty Turkish lira. Rustem had almost one hundred Turkish lira in his purse. He should be fine.

"This is Ani Topalian," said the clerk. "I will start the bidding at twenty lira."

Rustem's heart sank. He had hoped that the clerk wouldn't mention who she was. There were some who would like to own her simply for the prestige of it. Not to mention that she was very pretty.

"I will bid twenty," said Ali Fadil.

Rustem turned and looked at the man in surprise. Ali Fadil was a Marash jeweller too, and he and Hagop Topalian's unfriendly rivalry was well known.

"Twenty-five," said Rustem Bey.

He saw Mariam's head jerk up at the sound of his voice. She looked him in the eyes. He couldn't tell if it was with gratitude or anger.

He also saw that Ani was staring at him, her mouth slightly open with shock. He met her gaze and tried to convey to her that it would be fine.

"Thirty," said Ali Fadil.

Ani looked at Ali Fadil with unmitigated hate. She looked over to Rustem and frowned.

"Thirty-five," said Rustem Bey.

"Forty-five," said Ali Fadil.

Murmurs circulated throughout the room. Forty-five Turkish lira for a mere slip of a girl in a market overstocked?

"Fifty," said Rustem Bey, then held his breath. He could not bid more. He couldn't risk not having enough for Mariam.

"Do I have fifty-five?" said the clerk.

Silence.

"Sold to Rustem Bey for fifty Turkish lira."

Rustem walked up to the clerk and counted out the coins. Then he walked over to Ani and took her by the arm. He did it in such a way as not to hurt her, but he couldn't risk looking soft in this group. "Come with me," he said sternly.

Ani looked up at his face with confusion and hurt. It cut him to the quick that she doubted his motives.

"Mariam!" said the clerk.

She was the very last one called.

"I will start the bidding at ten," said the clerk.

"Twenty," said a voice from the threshold.

It was a familiar voice. Rustem Bey turned, then frowned in confusion. Captain Mustapha Sayyid? Why would he be bidding on a girl he already owned?

"Twenty-five," said Rustem Bey.

"Thirty-five," said Captain Sayyid.

He was driving up the bidding; that was his game, Rustem thought to himself. He turned and looked and saw that the Captain was looking right at him and smirking. He must know of my feelings for Mariam, thought Rustem Bey with a sinking heart. I hope I have enough.

"Forty-five," said Rustem Bey.

"Fifty," said the Captain.

"Fifty-five," said Rustem Bey, his heart in his mouth. He didn't have fifty-five Turkish lira in his purse, but he'd worry about that later.

"Sixty-five," said the Captain, a broad smile of triumph on his face.

The room was silent.

"Seventy-five," said Rustem Bey. He could feel a trickle of sweat dripping down the side of his face.

The Captain was silent.

"Sold to Rustem Bey for seventy-five Turkish lira," said the clerk.

No one said a word as Rustem, with Ani by his side, walked over to the clerk and opened his purse. "I don't have it all here," he said under his breath to the man. "But I can get you the rest if you wait."

The clerk looked at him and his brow wrinkled in annoyance. "These are cash transactions. You know that. Either you pay now, or the girl goes to the next highest bidder."

Rustem Bey looked around the room. The other men were watching him, but no one stepped forward to lend him money. Suddenly, he felt a hand in his, and then the heaviness of gold coins. He opened his palm. In it were two very old and valuable Ottoman gold coins. One was so rare that he had never seen one like it, except in paintings. "Use them," whispered Ani to him under her breath.

He held his palm out. The clerk's eyes widened with greed. "I'll give you your change," he said hastily, fearing that Rustem Bey might think twice about what he was doing. He counted out thirty of Rustem Bey's own Turkish lira and handed them back to him. With Ani holding onto his sleeve, he walked up to Mariam, smiling broadly.

Mariam's face was drained of all colour. She looked him in the eyes, and then her knees buckled and she collapsed on the ground. He scooped her up and carried her out the door. Ani followed close by his side, clinging onto his sleeve for her life.

Chapter Fourteen

It seemed fitting that the last person Kevork saw as they walked away from the orphanage the following day at dawn was Miss Younger. In spite of the fact that soldiers trained their bayonets on her, she stubbornly accompanied the deportees right to the orphanage gates.

"If you come any further, I will shoot you myself," said an angry Captain Sayyid. He pointed his rifle at her, and as far as Kevork could tell, the man was hoping she would take another step.

Miss Younger angrily brushed a tear from her cheek with the back of her hand, then stood at the open gate, less than a hand's breadth away from where the orphanage grounds ended and danger began.

Kevork looked over at Marta, who stood beside him. Her face was set with a fierce determination and her eyes were dry. That was good. Kevork did not want Captain Sayyid to know she was a girl.

In addition to the oxcart from the orphanage, which Mr. Karellian and Mr. Muller had expertly packed tight with food and supplies, there were two families waiting in the street.

One of the families had an oxcart, and household furniture was packed tightly and tied down. On the very top was a high-backed chair securely fastened with ropes looped around each leg and around the back. A very elderly Armenian woman sat in it. On her lap was a baby, blue in the face from crying. In addition to the old woman and baby in the oxcart, there were two adolescent girls, one younger boy, and a mother who looked to be in her thirties. These four were standing beside the cart, waiting for orders.

The other family consisted of a grandmother, a young boy, and a teenaged girl. They had no oxcart, and not even a donkey. All of their worldly goods had been bundled into large sacks of cloth and tied to their backs.

"Let's go," shouted Captain Sayyid. Then he spurred his stallion and led the way.

The oxcart with the grandmother and baby began to follow first after the Captain, then came the grandmother and children on foot. Behind them was the orphanage oxcart, driven by Mr. Karellian with Anna by his side. Behind the cart walked the other adult Armenians from the orphanage, and a few children deemed "adult," with Kevork and Marta at the very end.

The three groups of people could not move nearly as fast on foot and cart as Captain Sayyid did on horse, and soon the white horse was no more than a dot in the distance. Walking alongside the deportees were eight *zaptiehs* — civilian soldiers.

Each zaptieh was dressed in a secondhand Turkish army uniform, and each carried a rifle with a bayonet. With the Captain gone, the zaptiehs took over.

Kevork watched in anger as one of the zaptiehs prodded the grandmother on foot with his bayonet. "Move it," he said. "We don't have all day."

Just then, Mr. Karellian handed the reins to Anna and jumped down from the orphanage cart. He caught up to the grandmother. "Mairig," he said, "please take my place in our cart."

The woman looked up at him gratefully. Mr. Karellian held her bundle as she slipped it off her back.

"No stopping," yelled the zaptieh, and then he jabbed Mr. Karellian in the leg with his bayonet, ripping his trousers.

"This will help us go faster," said Mr. Karellian to the zaptieh.

"Then do it," said the soldier. "But don't stop walking."

Mr. Karellian slung the woman's load onto his own back, and then he took her by the elbow and led her to the oxcart. The zaptieh wouldn't let the cart stop even for a moment to let the old woman on, so she ended up walking beside it for several minutes. Anna wrapped the reins around her wrist to free up one hand, and then she reached down to the grandmother to help her up. The grandmother stumbled once, but then stepped up into the seat beside Anna.

Kevork watched as Mr. Karellian fell into step beside the woman's two grandchildren.

As they walked through the streets of Marash towards the southeastern gates, they created something of a sensation. Ordinary Turks came out of their houses to watch. Women stared out from latticed windows.

Kevork shook his head in disgust has he passed two men on the street corner, sipping lemonade and pointing at him. Did they consider this entertainment?

Suddenly, a young Turkish man ran out from nowhere and plunged into the middle of the deportation group. He picked up the granddaughter walking beside Mr. Karellian.

"I got one," he cried with excitement to a cluster of young men who were smoking and cheering him on. He threw the girl over his shoulder like a sack of cloth and ran down through a back street.

The grandmother let out a curdling scream. She tried to stand up in the cart, but Anna reached out and grabbed her sleeve, trying to get her to sit back down. The woman pushed Anna's hand away. She lost her balance and fell out of the cart, landing in the dirt on her hands and knees. Mr. Karellian ran over to her and tried to help her up. "Anoush," she cried. "Anoush." She raised one hand and pointed in the direction the man had run off with her granddaughter.

A zaptieh came over and pointed his rifle in her face. "Get up," he said, "or I will shoot you."

Mr. Karellian pulled on her arm to try to get her up, but the woman's legs buckled under her. She could sit up, but she couldn't stand.

The zaptieh shot her.

She crumpled into a heap.

Her grandson ran to her and wrapped his arms around her shoulders. "Mari Baji," he cried. "Please get up."

A group of women in veils clustered in the street, watching. One child, hiding behind the skirts of the women, ran forward and scooped up a stone. He threw it at the grandmother in the road. "Dirty Armenian traitor!" yelled the child.

A veiled woman stepped forward and grabbed the child's arm. "Stay out of it," she scolded.

The zaptieh walked up to the boy and his grandmother and prodded them both with the toe of his boot. "Either get up or die here," he said.

Mr. Karellian picked up the grandson. The boy was perhaps twelve years old and very strong. He flailed in Mr. Karellian's arms. "Let me go," he cried.

"Please be quiet," said Mr. Karellian. He continued walking away from the grandmother's body, her bundle on his back and her grandson struggling in his arms.

Kevork watched the scene in dismay. The zaptiehs would not put up with a scene like this for long. He turned to Marta and said, "Let us go up there."

The two of them walked quickly and caught up to where Mr. Karellian was struggling with the boy. "Come and walk with us," Kevork said to the boy.

The boy stopped his struggling long enough to look up at Kevork.

Kevork swallowed back tears as he looked into the young boy's eyes. Pain and loss were etched clearly there. Kevork felt as if he were looking into a mirror.

For some reason, the sight of Kevork and Marta settled the boy enough that Mr. Karellian could put him down. He walked between Marta and Kevork, and Mr. Karellian, limping, walked back to the oxcart and Anna helped him back up.

"What is your name?" Kevork asked the boy.

"Onnig," he said.

Onnig. The name brought back a flash of painful memories. Kevork wondered about Marta's brother, Onnig. And Anahid Baji, Ovsanna, and the children — Aram and Gadar. After only a few moments on the deportation march, Kevork's hopes of ever seeing them alive again had all but vanished.

He looked over at Marta and saw that her thoughts were his own. Furtively, so that the zaptiehs wouldn't see, he reached over and gave her hand a squeeze. She looked up at him and their eyes met. "We shall survive this," he said. "I promise."

By midday, they had passed through the southeastern gates of Marash and were marching out towards the desert. In the distance, Kevork could see other clusters of carts, donkeys, zaptiehs, and Armenians. As they walked, their little group fell into step and merged with the other deportation groups.

There were oxcarts and donkeys as far as the eye could see. The beasts and carts were stacked high with household items, food, and bedding. Beside the carts walked people: babies carried on the backs of young mothers; grandmothers and grandfathers so old and crippled that they had to be tied onto the carts like the furniture.

The eight Marash zaptiehs were joined by dozens of others, some on horses, most on foot.

Referring to these men pointing bayonets as "soldiers" was rather a stretch, Kevork realized. Rumour had it that the Young Turk government had emptied the prisons and issued uniforms and weapons to any criminal who wished to assist the army with the march. These scruffy "zaptiehs" were clearly distinguishable from regular army men.

Captain Sayyid sat astride his white stallion and wove up and down the deportation line, exhorting mothers with babies to walk faster and old people to stop dawdling. As he circled around the back of the line, Marta muttered something under her breath.

Kevork looked at her sharply. "Just make sure he doesn't hear you," he said.

"I want to know what he's done with my sister," said Marta.

Kevork didn't want to think about it.

CHAPTER FIFTEEN

It was the brightness of the light working its way in through the window that made Mariam finally wake up. There was an indistinct rumbling in the distance, and she could feel the ground shaking slightly beneath her. The first thing she saw when she opened her eyes was Ani, anxiously hovering above her. Ani was no longer in the dress covered with her mother's blood. Her face was washed, and her long hair was pulled up and braided into a coil on top of her head. She was wearing something pastel yellow and cottony.

Images jumbled back into Mariam's mind: the Captain, the auction, Rustem Bey … Mariam was so confused. "Are we safe?" she asked Ani.

"I believe so," said Ani. "Thank God you have awakened. I was beginning to think you were going to die, too." The words caught in her throat, and a sob escaped.

Mariam wanted to put her arms around the girl. Hadn't Herminé's dying request been for Mariam to look after Ani? Yet here the roles were switched. Mariam tried to sit up, but knives of pain shot through her stomach and she fell back down.

"Be careful," said Ani. "You passed out last night and are probably weaker than you realize."

Mariam turned her head to look at her surroundings. She was in a small room that had two intricately carved wooden doors. The walls were hung with deep crimson silk, and the enamelled black ceiling had a pattern on it similar to the swirls of carvings in the doors. She moved her hands to feel what it was that she was lying on. Something soft and slippery. She moved her woozy head just slightly. From the corner of her eye, she could see that she was lying on a feather-filled mattress covered with snow white silky sheets.

"Take a small sip," said Ani, holding a small crystal glass.

Mariam obeyed. The cool edge of the glass touched her lips and then a sweet peach-tasting liquid wet her tongue, chasing away the recent remnants of bile.

"It's called sherbet," said Ani. Then she set it down.

"Where are we?" asked Mariam.

"We are in the women's quarters of Rustem Bey's family home," said Ani. "The haremlik."

The word sent a shiver down Mariam's spine. She grabbed the blanket that covered her and pulled it to her chin. The strangeness of the cover made her momentarily forget her fear and she held it up to her face. It was pure white, and it was thick and fluffy, as if filled with feathers or wool. She folded it down and held up her arm. Like Ani, she was wearing something loose and yellow and cottony. She held her hand up to her face saw that the dirt and blood of the day before had been washed away.

Ani watched Mariam's dawning comprehension, and explained. "A servant brought a tub of hot water into the room. I stayed here on guard the whole time she sponged you clean."

The image brought a sad smile to Mariam's lips. Ani, a twelve-year-old girl from a pampered and wealthy home, had acted as a bath attendant to Mariam — a homeless orphan. A gasp of sadness filled her throat when the realization came: now Ani was the same as she. A homeless orphan. Yet she was nobody's child. She was in control. Mariam vowed to follow Ani's lead and become stronger and in control herself. It was the least she could do for Herminé's memory.

Mariam's eyes followed the source of light that had awakened her. It was streaming in through a large window that was covered with elaborately carved wooden latticework. The sight gave Mariam a jolt. How many times had she seen women's eyes staring out from latticed windows just like this? And now she was on the other side. What was that indistinct rumbling she heard?

"Please help me up," she said urgently to Ani.

Ani sat close to Mariam, holding one of her hands, and with one arm behind Mariam's back, she pulled her to a sitting position. Mariam grimaced in pain. "I must get to the window," she said.

Leaning on Ani for support, Mariam stood. Ani led her to the latticed window, and they both looked out.

Their window gave a bird's-eye view to the street below. From where Mariam stood, she could see right down into a single oxcart stacked high with household items. She looked down upon the heads of the people who were walking beside it, but from this angle she didn't recognize them. Behind the cart walked two men wearing filthy ripped Turkish army uniforms and brandishing rifles.

Mariam pressed her cheek up to the latticework to see if she could see further down the street. In the far distance, she could see more carts and people.

Ani stood beside her with her arm still around Mariam's waist. "I wish there was something we could do to help them," she murmured.

Mariam felt the same way. She felt guilty being in this room and relatively safe when her sister was most likely on the very street she was looking down at.

Without warning, one of the doors opened and a woman stepped through.

"Good morning, Hanim," said Ani, unwrapping her arms from Mariam's waist and bowing deeply to the intruder.

Mariam gripped the window frame for support and turned around.

Mariam had seen Turkish women at the public baths, and she had seen them fully veiled at the market. At the baths, women were either naked or loosely draped, and in the market or on the street, all that ever showed were the eyes and hands. Years ago, after the Adana massacres, Mariam had spent some time in Abdul Hassan and Amina Hanim's home. Amina Hanim was very conservative in her dress, even when she was unveiled in the house or working in the field. Mariam had assumed that all Turkish women were similarly conservative, but nothing could be further from the truth when it came to Guluzar Hanim.

Guluzar Hanim's hair was pulled back and braided, much like Ani's, but it was held in place with two emerald-encrusted combs. Mariam was mesmerized by the woman's face, which was painted. Lips and cheeks were rouged, and the eyes were accented with thin black lines. To Mariam, her face looked as if it were a beautiful painting on porcelain. The woman wore matching circlets of simple gold around her neck and wrists, and delicate gold chains studded with tiny jewels fell from her ears. Mariam had never seen a pierced ear before, and the thought of how the ear jewellery was fastened made her queasiness come back.

The woman wore a simple long tunic that fell straight down to her ankles. It was a deep emerald green silk brocade and it had hip-deep slits up both sides. Underneath, the woman wore trousers in a lighter weight material of the same colour, and on her feet were delicate jewelled slip-on flats.

Mariam let go of the window frame and tried to bow.

"Sit," said Guluzar Hanim in a frosty voice. And then she sat down on the bed and patted the spot beside her. Mariam sat. Ani stayed standing, looking anxiously on.

"My son wants to marry you, but I will not allow it."

Mariam was taken aback. She had not yet got bearings of her surroundings. Then this woman came bursting in and said such an incomprehensible thing.

Mariam's mouth opened, but no sound came out.

"It doesn't matter what you say," continued the Hanim. "I will make the decisions."

Mariam nodded. Not necessarily in agreement, but out of shock.

"You and Ani may stay here and recover as long as you obey me," said the woman. "But you are guests in my home and I do not want disruption."

"Hanim," Mariam said when she finally found her tongue, "thank you for your kindness."

The Hanim blinked. This wasn't what she had expected. She stood up. "Come through this doorway, down the hallway, and into the garden when you have freshened up," she said. "You can meet the other residents of the haremlik."

CHAPTER SIXTEEN

For Kevork and Marta, the deportation march became a drudgery of sorrow. One day blended into the next, and as the days passed, it got unbearably hot. Water and food became scarce. They were marched to Tel Abiad, a community on the banks of the Euphrates River, south of Urfa. Kevork was astonished to see thousands upon thousands of Armenian men, women, and children — half starved, with blistered feet, and open sores showing through the rags on their backs. Tel Abiad was a sort of transshipment centre. Armenian families had been rooted out of their homes from every part of Turkey and sent to this place in the desert.

One day Kevork said, "Look at that man over there. Does he look familiar?"

"No," said Marta. "Who do you think it is?"

"I am sure that is the Vartabed Garabed," said Kevork.

The Vartabed had been a true friend to Anna over the years. He had visited her about once a month at the orphanage, sometimes bringing her a book of prayers or a painted postcard showing a holy scene. Once when he was visiting, Kevork had noticed the sorry state of his boots and had offered to repair them, but the Vartabed refused, saying the precious leather would be better used for an orphan's feet than his own.

Kevork and Marta walked over to where the emaciated man was resting. It was indeed the Vartabed. Kevork knelt reverently in front of the startled priest and said, "God bless you, Very Reverend Father."

"Kevork!" exclaimed the Vartabed with delight. "I am relieved to see that you are alive."

The Vartabed looked over at Marta, but didn't recognize her in her boy's disguise. "Are you from Beitshalom too?" he asked.

"I am from Bethel," said Marta, looking him in the eyes.

"But ..." the Vartabed started. Then he squinted his eyes at her. "Yes, son," he said. "You are a healthy fellow, aren't you?"

Marta suppressed a sad smile. The Vartabed was a singularly bad liar.

Kevork was alarmed by the priest's appearance. He and Marta had been able to scavenge bits of food and had also been able to purchase a flask of water and some raisins with one of the gold coins that his father had left him from local desert Kurds who wandered through the deportees, selling food and water at outrageous prices.

It was quite apparent that the priest had not eaten for some time. He was a thin man anyway, but now he had wasted away so dramatically that it was a miracle he could still live. Kevork felt around in his pocket and pulled out a handful of raisins.

Kevork grabbed the priest's hand and opened his palm. He placed the raisins in it. "Eat, please," he said.

Father Garabed looked down at the raisins in his palm and frowned in confusion. Then he put them in his pocket.

"When were you deported?" asked Marta.

"My parish was one of the last groups of Armenians to leave Marash," replied the priest.

"Were the Hovsepians with you?" asked Marta.

"Nobody knows what happened to Ovsanna or Anahid Baji," replied the priest sadly. "They were not among the deportees when that area was rounded up."

"Do you think they may have escaped?" asked Kevork

"To where?" asked the priest. "Their only escape would be heaven."

Kevork looked over at Marta and saw that tears were filling her eyes. Being careful not to be seen, he quickly slipped his hand into hers and gave it a squeeze. "They're at peace," he said to her.

"What about the children?" asked Kevork. He didn't know whether he wanted to hear the answer, but for Marta's sake, he knew he had to ask.

"The two boys were taken into a Muslim home," said the Vartabed. "A good family. They will be raised Turkish, but they will live."

Kevork clenched his teeth in anger. The thought of Onnig and Aram being raised as Turks was almost more than he could stand. He hoped they were old enough to remember their past.

"What about Gadar?" asked Marta, a tremble in her voice. Ovsanna's little daughter had grown into a beautiful young girl.

The Vartabed sighed. "She lives," he said. "She is probably in Smyrna by now. She was bought by a white slave trader."

Marta's hand flew to her mouth in horror.

Kevork turned to her. "Perhaps she can escape. Smyrna is a trading centre on the sea." He knew that the possibility was remote, but he was desperate to say something encouraging to Marta.

Each day, the zaptiehs gathered together groups of deportees and took them in a different direction. Mr. Karellian was among the first of the orphanage group to be dispatched. Nobody ever came back. Each day, new deportees arrived to take their place.

Kevork and Marta separated themselves from the Marash deportees and made a point of blending in with the newest set of arrivals each day. Anna still walked behind the last stragglers in the column, urging them on, ensuring that they didn't get lost. Kevork had no idea what she managed to eat, but she refused all the food that he and Marta tried to give her. They kept the Vartabed Garabed with them, and he accepted the food they shared with him, but Kevork knew that he didn't eat it himself.

They tried to blend in, but they could delay their fate for only so long.

One morning, Kevork woke up with the sharp realization that his boots had been stolen. He looked over and saw that Marta's were gone, too. Bands of Kurds came through each night, stealing what they could, but it amazed Kevork that both he and Marta could have slept through such a key theft.

Kevork walked over to the body of an elderly Armenian man who had died through the night. He said a prayer for the man's soul, and then he crouched down and gently removed the man's shirt. He brought it back to where Marta was sitting, then tore it into strips. He handed her half of them. "Wrap your feet in these," he said.

As they wrapped their feet, one of the original zaptiehs from Marash approached them. "You're still here?" he said, poking Kevork in the ribs with his bayonet. "Get over with that group."

Kevork tied the last knot in his rag shoes and then got to his feet. He gave Marta one longing look, then walked over to the other group.

Kevork was alarmed to see Marta get up and walk over to him. Doing such a thing without being ordered to was like asking to be shot.

"Go away," Kevork whispered urgently.

"No," Marta whispered back. "I would rather die with you than alone."

Captain Mahmoud Sayyid happened to be walking past, and he overheard the last bit of the conversation. "You," he said, pointing to Marta. "Get back with the others."

She didn't move.

Kevork watched with dismay as the Captain ordered a zaptieh to restrain Marta. The man grabbed Marta by the shirt to pull her away. Her shirt tore open, exposing the fact that she wasn't a boy.

"I've found a girl!" cried the zaptieh.

The Captain watched with a satisfied smile on his face.

Kevork ran toward her, but the Captain drew out the sabre from his belt and struck Kevork's cloth-bound feet with the broad side. Kevork fell. The Captain held the point of the sabre to Kevork's back. "Move and you're dead."

The zaptieh who held Marta called out, "Friends, I've got a girl here!"

Just then, Anna came from out of nowhere. She grabbed a bayonet from a nearby zaptieh's hands and lunged at the man who was holding Marta. He saw her coming and ducked in the nick of time. Then the deportees and zaptiehs watched in horror as Anna lunged again, missing the zaptieh completely, but stabbing Captain Mahmoud Sayyid in the neck.

"That is for Mariam," she said fiercely.

Time stood still. Zaptiehs and deportees alike stared as the man collapsed, blood soaking his uniform. The zaptieh who was holding onto Marta was as mesmerized by the scene as everyone else.

"Run!" shouted Anna, breaking the spell. Marta pulled away from her captor just as his grip was regaining its strength. She dashed into the crowd.

The zaptieh's attention was now directed at Anna. "Infidel!" he cried. And with one swift movement, he pierced Anna's heart with his bayonet.

Then the zaptieh turned to deal with Marta. But she had vanished.

Kevork knew exactly where in the crowd she was hiding, but he didn't look. He willed himself to keep his eyes on his dying aunt. He said a silent prayer for her soul as she took her last breath. The zaptieh grabbed the Vartabed Garabed and marched him over to Kevork's group. "You can pay for that girl's insolence," he said.

Kevork and the priest and ten other men were led to the banks of the Euphrates River. As they stood on the rocky shore of the wide river in the middle of the desert, Kevork wondered what would happen next. He looked down into the water and it looked cool and inviting in the desert heat. Should he just jump in and end the torture? But then he thought of Marta. What if she lived and he didn't? What would that do to her? He thought of Anna and what she had sacrificed so Marta could live. Kevork decided that if he had to die, it would be to save someone else, not just to end his own pain.

CHAPTER SEVENTEEN

Guluzar Hanim walked out of Mariam and Ani's room and closed the door behind her.

"We cannot stay here," said Mariam. "I don't like that woman."

Ani sat down on the bed beside Mariam. "Where would we go?"

Mariam was silent.

"Rustem Bey is trustworthy," said Ani.

"Is he?" said Mariam.

"He has put his family in danger by bringing us here," said Ani. "We owe him our lives."

Mariam had been in such a haze of pain and shock that she had lost details about the auction and its implications. She shuddered at the thought of where she might be right now if it hadn't been for Rustem Bey.

"You are right," said Mariam. The whole situation was confusing, but she was beginning to feel guiltily grateful that she had been saved from the worst.

"Let us go to the garden," said Ani. And then she stood up and held out her hand to Mariam.

Mariam's stomach still hurt, but she willed herself to stand up straight. She did not want to appear weak in front of strangers.

"I was in the garden before," said Ani. "With my … my mother …" her eyes filled with tears.

The image of Herminé's bloodied corpse filled Mariam's mind. It seemed obscene that she and Ani were standing in this place — filled with luxuries and personally safe — while Ani's mother lay dead in a room across the city.

"We need to be strong," said Mariam, hugging Ani fiercely and trying to hide her own tears.

Ani took a deep breath. "Yes," she said.

When she stepped through the beaded curtains at the end of the hallway and entered the garden, Mariam was enveloped in the heady scent of flowers. It was as if she had walked into the Garden of Eden. There were lemon trees and grapevines, flowering shrubs and plants of every description and colour. Her first impression was that this garden was a place of relaxation and reflection.

There was a round pool with a fountain in the centre of the garden, and Mariam squeezed Ani's hand with sympathy when the girl gasped in sadness at the sight of it.

The fountain bubbled fresh, clean water, but Mariam's imagination was filled with the sight of three bloated corpses bobbing in another fountain across town. Ani's family.

In front of this fountain, there were three little girls sitting in a circle on the grass, playing with a kitten. One young woman in a long, blue tunic similar to the green one of Guluzar Hanim's sat on a bench close to the children. She balanced on her lap a small circular wooden frame that held a cloth of half-finished embroidery. Part of her attention was on her work, and the other was on the children.

Guluzar Hanim sat in a high-backed chair across from the younger woman, with a good view of the children. A servant girl stood behind her, waving a silk fan in rhythmic motion.

Mariam saw her turn her face towards her as she and Ani entered the garden.

Guluzar Hanim flicked her hand with an impatient motion at the servant, and the servant stopped fanning. She stood up and walked over to Mariam and Ani.

"Let me introduce you." She reached out and enveloped Mariam's hand in her own cool and firm one.

"Ede," said Guluzar Hanim. The young woman who had been watching the children looked up. "Come and meet our guests, dear," she said.

The younger woman set down her embroidery and stood up.

"This is my daughter, Ede Kadin," said Guluzar Hanim. "She is Rustem Bey's only full sibling."

Mariam bowed in greeting, as did Ani.

"This is Mariam," said Guluzar Hanim dryly. "The girl your brother keeps on talking about."

Ede grinned. "I'm glad to finally meet you," she said. The girl's honey-coloured skin and kind brown eyes made her look strikingly similar to Rustem. She wore her long, straight hair parted in the middle and flowing down her back.

It gave Mariam a start to think that Rustem Bey talked about her to his mother and sister. She had barely thought of him from one day to the next, and yet all of these people here knew about her.

Mariam bowed to Ede.

Guluzar Hanim motioned towards the three children playing with the kitten. "Two of those children are Rustem's half sisters: Ayesha and Leyla," she said dismissively. "Nura Hanim — Rustem Agha's third wife — is their mother. The other girl is Taline: an Armenian orphan Ede picked up."

Mariam was taken aback by the way she said it. "Picked up" like a stray cat? she wondered. She regarded the three girls. They were all dressed with equal richness. There was much she had to learn.

A light jingling announced that someone else had entered the garden. Mariam turned. A young, breathlessly beautiful Turkish woman entered. This woman also wore a sumptuous silk brocade tunic with high slits in the side and matching trousers underneath. Like Guluzar Hanim, this woman wore green. But it was a deeper, richer green. Her hair had been hennaed red and was wrapped in a coil on the top of her head. Mariam had thought that Guluzar Hanim was beautiful and elegant, but this woman was even more so.

Mariam looked over to Guluzar Hanim and saw that her lips were smiling, but her eyes were flashing with unmasked hate. "Nura Hanim," she said in a controlled and pleasant voice. "How nice of you to join us. This is Mariam, the Armenian girl."

Mariam bowed to her.

"And of course you know Ani."

Ani bowed.

Nura Hanim smiled. "Why don't you two take a walk around the garden with me while Guluzar Hanim rests her weary legs?"

The interchange between the two women seemed so petty to Mariam. Her imagination was consumed with the possible fates of Marta and Kevork, her grandmother, brother, and others. Did these women not know what was happening outside?

"Come," said Nura Hanim, looping one hand through Mariam's arm and the other through Ani's. "I want to check my roses."

Mariam pasted a smile on her face. It was so hard to pretend that the state of this woman's roses was of any interest to her, yet she didn't need any more enemies. As they walked through the garden, Mariam noticed the high walls on all four sides. This might be the Garden of Eden, but it wasn't a garden that could be easily escaped. The happy sound of children laughing and the woman's inane chatter didn't fully muffle the sounds of the deportation operations beyond the walls. Mariam knew that she was somewhat safe, but she felt just as much a prisoner as the people beyond the walls.

After the walk around the garden, the ladies sat together on deep cushions and a low table was placed before them. A sumptuous array of cakes and preserved fruits was laid out by two servant girls who Mariam sus-

pected were Armenian. Mariam sipped her glass of sherbet, but she didn't have the stomach to eat. Her stomach still hurt from the Captain's punch, and her heart
ached for the people outside. She looked across the
table at Ani and noticed that she too was putting on an
act of contentment, but she hadn't touched her food.

CHAPTER EIGHTEEN

There was a sound in the water and Kevork looked up. A wooden dinghy navigated with a long pole by an elderly man approached the shore. The dinghy was made of planks of wood lashed together with rope, then tied onto twenty or more inflated goat skins for buoyancy. Kevork was amazed that the craft didn't capsize.

The boatman was Kurdish. Kevork knew this by the man's *salvar* — trousers tight from ankle to knee and then billowing out to enormous fullness above the knee. The man wore a tunic with a wide blue sash and a tasselled fez on his head.

The elderly Kurd guided his craft to the shore, then waited with a bored expression on his face while the zaptiehs prodded with bayonets the dozen men onto the planks of wood. Once they were all on, the man dipped his long wooden pole into the rocks at the bottom of the river and pushed out.

Kevork squinted his eyes and looked at the shore as long as he could, but he didn't get a last glimpse of Marta.

The Vartabed and the other men sat down on the dinghy, and so Kevork stepped gingerly to where they were and sat next to the priest. Kevork stared out at the water, mesmerized by its coolness. Others before him must have been seduced by the water as well, because as they travelled deeper into the desert, the Euphrates was studded with bobbing corpses, bloating in the heat of the sun. Kevork shuddered, then turned his head and looked at the Vartabed instead. The priest's face was serene, and his lips moved in prayer.

Before he knew it, the dinghy bumped into the other side of the Euphrates.

The boatman lifted his long stick from the water and prodded the men to make them hurry off his dinghy. Once they had all stumbled onto dry, rocky ground, he stuck the stick back in the water and manoeuvred his craft back over to the other side. Kevork marvelled at the man's industry. To the boatman, this was just a job: get as many people over to Deir-Ez-Zor, a city in the middle of the Syrian desert, as quickly as possible. Kevork wondered if he was paid by the head.

There was a different group of zaptiehs on this side of the Euphrates, and they herded the group from the dinghy over to one side, and then stood and waited for more people to arrive. Kevork watched as a woman with a baby and two children, an elderly woman, and a handful of men stepped off the next dinghy. Marta was not in the group. He didn't know whether to be happy or sad about that. Perhaps she had a chance to escape? The possibility was remote, but he clung to it.

The zaptiehs waited for several more dinghies to arrive, and Kevork watched, but still no Marta.

"It's time to go," yelled a zaptieh. Kevork stood up, then helped the Vartabed to his feet. And they marched in the direction the bayonets prodded.

They marched into the depths of the desert. When it got dark, they slept in the sand. When Kevork woke the next morning, his shirt with its coin had been stolen. He walked for that whole day in nothing but trousers and the tattered rags around his feet. The sun beat down on his head and back and his skin reddened and blistered.

That night, he was too sore to lie down and sleep, and so he sat, hands on knees. He dreamt that Marta was with him. He thought he could hear her whispering in the dark. But when he woke up the next morning, he was lying on his side. His trousers and his last gold coin had been stolen. The other deportees were in the same situation as he. Kurds would come in the night and steal whatever they could, whether from corpses or soon-to-be corpses.

They arrived at the town of Aneh in the Syrian desert and rested a day. There they met up with other walking skeletons. Then they were driven like a herd of animals all the way back to Deir-Ez-Zor.

They were being marched in circles.

Every death affected the Vartabed as if it were the only one he had ever witnessed. At night, the priest would sprinkle a bit of desert sand on each new corpse and whisper a prayer. The zaptiehs laughed at him. And while the Vartabed became more sensitive, Kevork's emotions shut down. When he thought about it, Kevork could trace back this change of heart to the day he lost Marta. It hurt too much to think of her, and when he saw others die, it made him think of her. The only way he could function was to not think.

Once, he walked past the corpse of a mother whose baby still whimpered feebly in her arms. The Vartabed wanted to save the child, but Kevork didn't. Save her for how long? Wasn't it better that the baby die with her mother's arms wrapped around her in love? How many grandmothers had he walked past who had simply given up — sitting at the side of the road waiting to die? Sometimes wraithlike children would sit listlessly beside the old women. Kevork knew what had become of their parents.

No matter how many Armenians died, it seemed that there were always more to kill. The roads were littered with corpses, yet more deportees arrived each day. Kevork couldn't understand why the Turks didn't just shoot them all and be done with it.

These wretched walking skeletons were herded up again and made to walk all the way north to el-Jezireh, in the very heart of the desert wasteland.

Hunger and thirst, combined with burning days and freezing nights, felled the deportees one by one. Kevork noted with detachment the effect of sun and heat on the bodies of the dead. During the first day or so after death, a body would swell and puff up. After that, it would deflate, then cook in the sun. Bodies that had been exposed for several days would ooze oil that would leach into the sand as the body decomposed. As time went on, the skin dried like leather and shrunk from the bone. Kevork had plenty of opportunity to observe this process as he and the other survivors were forced to step over the bodies of the dead.

Kevork and the Vartabed miraculously clung to life. Each night, as the priest gave the newly dead their last rites, Kevork would collapse in exhaustion and sleep wherever he fell. In the morning a zaptieh would kick them awake and force them on their march to nowhere.

After ten days of marching into the desert, the thousands of survivors had dwindled to about a hundred — a handful of starving and disease-ridden humanity. Any food or water was long gone. The cool blue wetness of the Euphrates River sparkling just beyond reach was an added torture. Crazed with thirst, each day one or more of the deportees made a run for the river. The ones who didn't make it were shot by zaptiehs who were grateful for the target practice. The ones who did make it died in agony as their stomachs swelled and burst with the sudden intake of salt water. Over the days of marching in circles past the Euphrates, more and more Armenians, desperate for just a taste of water even if it meant sure death, ran to the river.

One morning, Kevork awoke to a blood-curdling cry. "Chechen bandits."

The marauders fell upon the pathetic group and hacked away at them with knives and sabres. Kevork was clubbed over the head, and he fell to the ground. By the time the Chechens were finished, the hundred or so survivors were reduced to twelve: eight men and four women. Four of the men were lashed together and led up a hill out of sight. There was gunfire. And then silence. A few moments later, the Chechens came back.

One of the Chechens pulled Kevork to a standing position, and then he lashed Kevork and the Vartabed to the two remaining men. They were led up the same hill. When they got to the top, the Vartabed fell to his knees in prayer. Because they were lashed together so tightly, Kevork and the other two men fell to their knees, too.

The Vartabed addressed one of the Chechens. "I would like to administer the sacrament of the dying to these men and myself before you execute us."

The bandits were taken aback. Then they fell to their knees in front of the priest and asked for understanding. "We are only following government orders," one man cried. "And the hand of God directs the Turkish government."

"May God forgive your sins," said the Vartabed Garabed.

Then he administered the last rites. When he was finished, he scooped a handful of sand and held it up to heaven. "This is the Body and Blood of our Lord Jesus Christ," he said, and he placed a single grain of sand on the tongue of each doomed man.

When the Vartabed had finished, the Chechens untied the men, then lined them in a row. The Chechens did not blindfold them, and so Kevork found himself staring down the barrel of a rifle. Then he heard the deafening sound of gunfire.

One by one, the men fell as the bullets hit. The one intended for Kevork whizzed past his abdomen, grazing his skin. He screamed and fell to the ground as he had seen the others do. With none of the prisoners left standing, the Chechens left. Within minutes, another group of Chechens came to finish off the work begun by their brothers. They clubbed Kevork over the head and he lost consciousness.

CHAPTER NINETEEN

One thing that Mariam had trouble getting used to in the haremlik was the lack of privacy. The room that she and Ani shared had two doors in it, but no locks. At various times of the day, Guluzar Hanim, Ede, or Nura Hanim would burst through unannounced. Sometimes it would simply be to walk through to another room, but at other times it was to sit and chat. Everyone knew everyone else's business.

Living in an orphanage, and a crowded house before that, Mariam was used to having lots of people around. But at Anahid Baji's or even at the orphanage, there was a deep sense of the individual. Here in the haremlik, it was as if no one had the right to private thoughts.

So Mariam was surprised when she heard a tap-tapping on the door one day as she sat alone in the room, staring out the latticed window. Who would be knocking? she wondered. She walked over to the door and opened it, and there stood Rustem Bey.

"We need to talk," he said.

Mariam opened the door wide and stepped aside so he could enter, her face flushing hot at the thought of being alone with him in a room where the main piece of furniture was a bed. Rustem seemed to understand her discomfort, and he took two pillows from the bed and positioned them on the floor facing each other, and then he sat down on one of them. Mariam sat down on the other.

"I am sure the ladies have told you that I like you," he said.

Mariam looked up at him and smiled. "It seems to be all they talk about," she said.

"I wanted to formally have my family ask your family for your hand in marriage," Rustem Bey continued, "but then the deportations began."

Mariam could feel the heat of embarrassment on her face. She looked down at her hands.

"So I must ask you this," said Rustem. "It doesn't matter how you answer. You are welcome to the safety of my house as long as you wish."

Mariam stayed silent, dreading the question.

"Would you want to marry me if you were asked?" he asked.

Mariam's mouth filled with tears. No words came out. She shook her head no.

Rustem Bey's shoulders sagged in defeat. "I thought that would be your answer," he said.

Mariam took a gulp of air, then wiped the tears from her eyes. "It comes at the wrong time," she said. "I cannot think of marriage when death surrounds us."

"Then you may have said yes in different circumstances?" he asked.

"I must be honest," said Mariam. "I could not live like this, sequestered in a garden and a set of rooms, with nothing more than sweets and kittens to keep me occupied. I respect you, but I don't like this way of life."

A frown of hurt formed on Rustem Bey's face. "It is wealth, not culture, that keeps our women idle. Wealthy Armenian women are no different."

Mariam could have blurted out that wealthy Armenian women were mostly dead or worse right now, or marching towards the desert, but she held her tongue. "I like you as a friend," she said. "And I thank you for saving my life."

Rustem's frown disappeared. He reached out and grabbed her hand. "I will always be your friend." He looked into her eyes and said, "I am sorry that you are not happy here."

Mariam regarded him with surprise. "Happiness is not important right now," she said. "I am alive. But when I look outside, I see Armenians being rounded up. Deported. I feel guilty being here. And I feel useless."

Rustem Bey was quiet for a moment, and then he said, "I've been thinking the same thing."

"You have?"

"Yes," he said. "I feel useless, too. I asked Miss Younger if I could do something to help, but she told me no. To only keep supplying food. I would like to do more."

Mariam squeezed his hand. "Could you take me there?" she asked.

"To the orphanage?" asked Rustem Bey. "You would be arrested."

"But if I were fully veiled and accompanied you on a food delivery, couldn't I go?"

Rustem Bey nodded. "If you wish," he said. "But it would be risky. You would have to pose as my odalisque, and you would have to let people think you had converted."

"I could do that," said Mariam.

"Even with Miss Younger," said Rustem Bey. "If word got out that I was harbouring Armenians, my house would be burnt down, you would be executed before my eyes, and then I would be killed."

"I understand," said Mariam firmly. "I will play the part."

Mariam found the heavy veiling oddly cool and comfortable as she took Rustem's hand and he helped her step up to the wooden bench on the oxcart. It was piled high with flour and raisins and olives and other foodstuffs. Rustem pulled himself up beside her and then took the reins.

The oxen walked slowly through the streets of Marash, and Mariam looked out of the narrow opening between her head covering and the yashmak on her face to see streets that no longer looked familiar. There was a quiet desolation to the place, as if removing the Armenians had cut the heart out of the city.

Mariam swallowed back tears as the mighty gates of the orphanage appeared. Rustem handed her the reins, and then he hopped down from the cart and rang the bell. Mariam's mind was filled with the image of the first time she had come here so many years ago. Then, it was Paris who had answered the door. Little Paris, who was killed by Captain Sayyid. And it was Mariam's fault.

This time, the door was opened by Parantzim, the new orphan who had arrived just days before the deportation. Mariam was pleased to see that the girl smiled broadly and had a healthy glow about her.

"Is Miss Younger in?" asked Rustem.

Parantzim's eyes darted from Rustem Bey to the lady in veils, and then to the cart loaded with food. "She will be happy to see you, sir," she said. "Let me take you."

"Would you like to ride on the cart?" asked Rustem.

"I would," was the enthusiastic reply.

Parantzim was so light that Rustem picked her up without effort and sat her beside Mariam.

Without speaking to Parantzim, Mariam tugged on the reins and the oxen walked forward. Rustem walked beside the cart.

They encountered Miss Younger, head bent down in thought, walking towards her office. She looked up in surprise when she heard the cart approach. Mariam noticed her eyes rest first on Parantzim, and then on Mariam — an unrecognizable lady in veils.

"Rustem Bey," Miss Younger said. "How good of you to bring more supplies. I was just about to put in another order."

"These are a donation," said Rustem.

"Thank you," said Miss Younger.

"May we speak to you in private?" asked Rustem Bey.

"Certainly," she replied. "Let us go to my office."

Rustem lifted Parantzim down, and she scampered away. Then he held out his hand for Mariam. The two followed Miss Younger in silence.

Once the office door closed behind them, Mariam lifted up her veil. Miss Younger gasped. "You're safe," she cried. "Thank God." Her eyes darted from Rustem to Mariam in confusion, trying to ascertain the relationship.

Rustem Bey did not illuminate her. They sat. "What is happening with the orphanage?" he asked.

Miss Younger walked over to the other side of the desk and sat down in her chair with a sigh. "Every day," she said, "officials come with one excuse or another to take away more orphans."

"But I thought you had been assured of their safety," said Rustem.

"I have been. But Turkish orphanages have been set up, and these children are to go to them," she said.

"These children cannot go to Turkish orphanages," said Mariam. "They will forget that they're Armenian."

"But they will be alive," said Rustem Bey.

"Perhaps," said Miss Younger. "We cannot be sure what the motivations are. I have been ordered back to Germany, but I will not go."

"What about the other missionaries?" asked Mariam.

"Some have already left, but a few are staying. I have sent telegrams to the American Embassy, and I am hoping that American and Canadian missionaries will arrive here to keep this orphanage open. In the meantime, I am trying to keep the children safe."

"As you know," said Rustem Bey, "I have offered to help."

"I cannot let you risk your life to hide Armenians," replied Miss Younger firmly.

"But what if Mariam and I adopted a child?" asked Rustem Bey. "Would that be acceptable?"

Miss Younger looked in confusion from Mariam to Rustem.

Rustem Bey stayed silent.

"Trust us," was all that Mariam would say.

"Which child?" asked Miss Younger.

Without hesitation, Mariam answered, "Parantzim."

CHAPTER TWENTY

Kevork was awakened by the sound of buzzing flies. The sun had set and the air was chilly, but Kevork wasn't cold. The bodies of the other men kept him warm. He was stiff and sore but amazed to be living. Kevork pushed off the body that had fallen on top of him. He sat up, but was dizzy from loss of blood. He looked down at the bodies surrounding him and found the Vartabed. He reached out and touched his cheek and was shocked to feel that it was warm. Could it be possible that the Vartabed had survived too? Kevork placed his fingers on the side of the priest's neck. Yes, there was a fluttering of life. Kevork gently slipped his hands around the priest's body to find out where he had been shot.

"Do not worry about me, Kevork," murmured the priest faintly. "I am anxious to meet my maker." And then his head lolled over to one side. Kevork felt for a heartbeat in the priest's neck but couldn't find one.

Kevork thought that he was deadened to all emotion, but the death of Vartabed Garabed hit him hard.
His body convulsed with dry heaving sobs. The
Vartabed Garabed was such a good man. Why had he
died while Kevork lived? Kevork sprinkled a bit of sand
on the priest's body and said a prayer.

Kevork checked on the two other men. One was
dead from a bullet between the eyes. The other man was
breathing. Kevork pulled him away from the corpses.

Kevork forced himself to stand up and get his
bearings. He didn't want to leave the other survivor to
go looking for shelter. Kevork was afraid that the man
would gain consciousness while he was gone, look
around at the other corpses, then give up and die. So
instead of looking for shelter, Kevork mounded sand
as support and warmth on one side of him, and then
he huddled up closely to the man's other side. Kevork
fell asleep, not knowing if either of them would be
alive at dawn.

It was the stillness that awoke him early the next morning. Since the first day of the deportation, Kevork had
accustomed himself to being wakened by groans and
screams of other prisoners as they were kicked awake.
He had always tried to scramble to his feet at the first
scream to avoid the kicks. But this morning everything
was too quiet. He opened his eyes a tiny bit in the bright
sunlight and moved his head from side to side, then
struggled into a sitting position and touched the man
beside him. Still warm. But he wouldn't waken.

Kevork fell back in exhaustion and drifted into an uneasy sleep. He dreamt that Marta was still with him, touching his cheek tenderly. He opened his eyes. Two Kurdish children in rags were trying to pry open his mouth. Overhead were the vultures.

"I will not die now," Kevork cried out loud. The children shrieked and ran away. Kevork sat up and looked around. The man was still lying beside him. Kevork felt for a pulse. Nothing.

Kevork wandered aimlessly looking for shelter — any kind of shelter. He walked past countless Armenians, all dead.

Then he saw a shadow. If only he could get to the shadow, maybe he would be safe. With ragged feet on scorching sand, Kevork walked towards the shadow. When he got there, it was gone. He squinted his eyes and looked up at the ball of fire in the sky. "Will you kill me today?" he asked the sun. But he didn't die. He kept on walking towards imaginary shelters that would dissolve in the sand as he approached them. Kevork's tongue was thick and his throat was parched. Death would be a relief when it finally came.

Then something strange happened. There was something up ahead — and as Kevork trudged forward, it did not disappear! He thought for sure it was another trick, but he walked towards it anyway.

It was a shack. Or at least it had been, years or decades ago. The desert had eroded it down to the hardened mud floor. Only a bit of straw and mud wall still stood. During the middle of the day, this ruin would provide almost no shelter from the burning sun. But now, past noon, there was a shadow already forming under one of the walls. Kevork collapsed into the meagre shade and fell into an exhausted sleep.

He woke up with a start.

A Kurdish child in rags, giggling. She threw a stone at Kevork.

It smacked him near his eye, but he was too weak to protest. When the child noticed Kevork was awake, she ran away.

Kevork lost all concept of time. It could have been hours or days that passed. Or maybe it was only minutes. His body was on fire with fever and it swelled up. When Kevork held up his arm to look at it, he remembered all the bloated corpses. Is this what it feels like to die? he wondered. Maggots feasted on his wounds. He had not consumed a drop of water or a crumb of food for as long as he could remember. It puzzled Kevork that he could possibly be alive, but then, he thought, maybe he was dead and just didn't know it.

Kevork heard a slight movement beside him and he opened one eye. An Arab boy in loose flowing robes was standing there, staring at him. He ran away when he saw that Kevork was awake. The next time Kevork opened his eyes, the child was back, this time with a wizened old Arab woman in tow. Kevork was surprised to see that her face was uncovered. In Marash, all Muslim women covered their faces. The woman bent down and wet Kevork's lips with water from a goatskin. She said something in Arabic to the child, who ran away, coming back almost immediately with some Arab men.

She stood up to face the men, hands on hips. There was an argument. Kevork listened through a haze of delirium. Then Kevork was dragged on a blanket to a cluster of tents in the sand.

The next thing Kevork remembered was the sensation of soft, woollen blankets beneath his burnt skin. The few rags that he had been wearing were gone, and his body had been washed. He could feel the stickiness of some sort of ointment on his back. His body was covered with a soft, loose cloth, but he was naked underneath. He could see the faint outline of the sun trying to beat down on him through a tent of tightly woven wheat-coloured cloth. Through a haze of delirium, Kevork felt the cool firmness of a clay cup touching his lips, and then the heavenly moisture of a tepid meat broth. The cup was offered briefly each time. Just enough for a tiny sip.

Kevork had no sense of time. It was like slowly waking up from a bad dream. As his consciousness surfaced, more details of his circumstances emerged. He could see the leathery brown hand that held the clay cup. The wrist disappeared into a fold of linen. He looked up and saw the wizened Madonna face of the woman who had saved him.

Kevork tried to speak, but she held up the palm of her hand as if to stay "stop." And then, in Armenian, she said, "Rest. You are safe."

Chapter Twenty-One

Guluzar Hanim watched through the latticed window in her own luxuriously appointed bedroom when her son's empty cart returned later that day. What infuriated her even more than the wanton giving away of food was the fact that there was yet another stray Armenian orphan sitting on the bench of the oxcart between Rustem and that Mariam. "What a bad influence she is," she muttered under her breath. "I must look after this immediately."

Rustem Bey had barely driven the cart back to the stable when a veiled servant girl came to inform him that his mother desired a cup of coffee with him in her room.

"Tell her that I will see her in an hour."

"I am sorry, sir," said the girl, looking down at the ground. "I have been told that you are to come with me now."

He handed the reins to a stable boy and followed the servant.

His mother was reclined on a divan in her bedroom. She was fully dressed, but her eyes were closed, and there was a damp towel draped across her forehead.

"Mother, are you all right?" asked Rustem Bey. His voice feigned alarm, but he knew that his mother was fine. The damp cloth across the forehead was more an indication that she wanted attention than illness on her part.

"I have a headache," she said. "I dreamed that this house was overrun with Armenians."

Rustem smiled inwardly. She had been watching through the window. "I brought an Armenian child to keep Mariam company. She is very lonely."

"You seem to be spending too much time with her yourself," replied Guluzar Hanim.

"Is there anything wrong with me having an odalisque?" he asked.

His mother took the damp cloth from her forehead and she opened her eyes. "So you have abandoned thoughts of marrying her?" she asked hopefully.

"Yes, mother," he replied wearily. "I have." That it was Mariam who had abandoned the thoughts was none of his mother's business. That she was not his odalisque was also not her business. If everyone thought she was his odalisque, he could visit her in privacy when he wanted.

"But you must be married," said Guluzar Hanim. "And the sooner, the better."

Rustem Bey was too angry to respond. The last thing he wanted to think about right now was marrying someone else.

"It has been arranged," continued Guluzar Hanim. "Halah Mustapha will be your bride."

The news of Rustem Bey's upcoming wedding circulated the haremlik in no time. Mariam was initially hurt. Hadn't Rustem just asked her to marry him? Was he so fickle as to choose someone else so quickly? But when she saw the look of triumph on Guluzar Hanim's face over the dinner table that evening, she understood. This was in every way an arranged marriage. It was for the best, she thought. Perhaps this new bride would bring Rustem Bey the happiness he deserved.

Mariam found life in the harem to be exceedingly tedious. The days were spent playing with the kitten, sipping tea, and eating sweets. None of the women except she and Ani could read, and even so, there were no books. Ani occupied most of her days sitting in the corner of the room, working on a large piece of embroidery. It worried Mariam that she rarely went out to the garden and didn't eat much nourishing food. She would nibble on sweets and sip sweetened tea, and that was about it. She was becoming paler and thinner by the day, although her cheeks were bright pink and her eyes were bright.

Parantzim adapted to harem life right away. She and the other young girls bonded immediately. The peals of their laughter and the thumping of their tiny feet could be heard all through the day as they played one game after another. Even Guluzar Hanim came to tolerate Parantzim, although she insisted she be called by her Turkish name: Sheruk-rey-ah.

Mariam spent long hours in the garden, walking around and around and around. She felt like an animal in a cage, but the walking settled her mind. She had heard whispers from the Armenian servants that the people who had been deported had been forced to walk around and around and around in the desert until they died.

She also set up writing lessons for the four little girls. "This is allowed," remarked Guluzar Hanim, happening upon them mid-lesson one day, "as long as you stick to teaching them in Turkish."

Mariam taught all four girls in Turkish, but it was Armenian folk tales in Turkish that she used for the writing lessons. She also took Parantzim and Taline aside whenever she was able, and she would tell them Bible stories in whispered Armenian. She tried to get Ani to sit with them during the lessons, but Ani rarely did.

One day Ede — Rustem's sister — came up to Mariam as she taught the younger girls. "Could I sit in too?" she asked timidly.

"Of course," said Mariam.

Even after the little girls tired of the lessons, Ede would stay on. "I would have loved to go to school," Ede confided in her.

Mariam was surprised at this. She had assumed that Ede and the others were happy with their existence.

Chapter Twenty-Two

The woman brought in a clay basin and strips of clean rags. She drew back the cloth that was covering Kevork and looked at the bullet wound in his side. She dipped one rag into the liquid. Kevork wrinkled his nose at the pungent smell.

"Goat urine," she said.

She gingerly draped the urine-soaked rag on the bullet wound. Kevork gasped in pain. She left it there for a moment or two, then took it off. It was covered with bits of blackened crusty blood.

"It is not healing," she said, frowning.

She moistened another rag in the vile liquid, and as she draped it on the wounded area, Kevork passed out.

When he awoke, Kevork thought he was seeing double. The wizened Madonna face was gazing into his with concern. "We must try something else."

Beside her was another old woman. This woman was frailer looking, but her black-brown eyes sparkled with intelligence. "Hold his shoulders," she said.

Kevork's Madonna repositioned herself so that his head was resting on her lap. She looped her arms under his armpits and held him tight.

The smaller woman took a wad of clean rags and said to Kevork in Arabic, "Bite on this," then she placed it between his teeth. She flipped the cloth down and gently prodded the wound with her fingertips. Kevork groaned in pain.

She looked up at him and met his eyes. "The bullet is still in there," she said. "It is surrounded by pus. It won't heal until we get the bullet and the pus out."

Kevork nodded, then clenched his teeth on the cloth. The last thing he remembered before passing out was feeling the woman's hands pushing hard at his wound, as if she were squeezing a massive pimple.

When he woke up, the second woman was gone, but Kevork's Madonna was still there, sitting in the corner, mending garments. Her eyes brightened when she noticed he was awake.

"The bullet came out," she said, smiling.

She set down her mending and walked over to him. She pulled down the linen and showed him his side. The skin was healthy and pink. No longer was the wound swollen and ragged with putrid edges. Now there was a hole the size of a coin. The edges were clean and straight and looked freshly cut. A thin healthy scab was already starting to form.

The sight of it made Kevork feel woozy. He closed his eyes and lay back down.

He felt the cool dryness of the woman's hand on his forehead. "The fever is gone," she said. "You'll be feeling better soon."

What woke Kevork the next time was the absence of pain. The woman wasn't sitting at his feet, doing her mending. He sat up, then marvelled at the fact that he could sit up. He flipped back the linen that covered him. His whole abdomen was wrapped in clean white linen, held together with strips of cloth tied in knots. He gingerly poked at the cloth right above the bullet wound and was amazed that there was only a dull ache. He looked around him and saw that there was a wooden tray covered with a square of cloth sitting on the ground beside him. He removed the cloth. A jug filled with water, an empty cup, and a bowl filled with something white and gooey.

Kevork was so weak that lifting up the jug took a real effort. The water tasted like nectar as it wet his lips. He scooped a small bit of the goo with his fingers and placed it on his tongue. An image flashed in his mind: the Vartabed and his last Communion of sand. Kevork let the food dissolve on his tongue and then he washed it down with a sip of water. He said a silent prayer for the soul of the Vartabed, then said another for the thousands of other lost souls. And he prayed for Marta.

The tent flap opened and Kevork squinted at the sudden beam of light. When the tent flapped closed again, Kevork could see. His Madonna had returned.

"You're looking healthy," she said, grinning.

"Thank you for saving my life," said Kevork.

"I wish I could have saved more," replied the woman. "We saw thousands of Armenians being marched in the desert, past our settlement in Rakki, but the soldiers were watching us, not letting us intervene."

"How is it that you speak Armenian?" asked Kevork.

The woman's eyes sparkled. "I was born Armenian," she replied. "These Arabs saved me, much like I did you, many years ago."

"Saved you from what?" asked Kevork.

"The earlier massacres," replied the woman. "In 1896, the Sultan ordered the Armenians to be killed. I was not much older than you at the time."

Kevork blinked in wonder. The woman was not yet forty.

"My Armenian name was Zarouhi," she continued. "But the Arabs call me Huda — a better Muslim name. Please call me that."

"Thank you, Huda, and my name is Kevork."

"Kevork ... Kevork ..." said Huda. "Here, you shall be Khedive, agreed?"

Kevork nodded. He had been reborn.

"Now, promise me something," Huda said.

"Anything."

"You must not leave this tent until I tell you it is safe."

"Are there still Turks in the area?"

"We are being patrolled regularly," replied Huda. "And they will kill us all if they find you."

So Kevork stayed in the tent. Huda brought him food and sat with him when she had the time. Kevork was strong enough to stand, and so he would alternate from sleeping, to sitting, to standing in the middle of the tent — the only place that was tall enough for his full height. It was a boring existence, but the boredom was like a balm to Kevork's soul.

Kevork lost all sense of time. His side healed and the wrappings came off. Huda brought him a length of cloth to hide his nakedness. The hair on his head grew long and shaggy, and when Kevork felt his face, he realized that it was covered with a beard. It was days or weeks later when Huda announced that it was now safe for him to leave the tent. She laid out some Arab-style clothes. After so much time in solitude, Kevork was almost afraid to go outside.

"Are the deportations over?" he asked Huda.

"No," she said. "They've simply moved on. Dress. I will be back for you shortly."

After she left and the tent flap closed, Kevork looked at the clothing she had left him. There was a *thwab* — a loose flowing linen robe — and there was also large square of cloth known as a *guttrah* and a length of rope made of goat's hair and sheep's wool. There were also sturdy leather sandals. He drew the loose robe over his head and was pleased with how cool and comfortable it felt.

Kevork had seen guttrahs worn by Arabs and he had a good idea of how it would go on. He folded the cloth on a diagonal, making a large triangle. He placed the triangle on his head with the long straight side over his forehead. One corner was pointed towards the back and the other two were positioned over each shoulder. He took the length of rope and wrapped it around his head twice, tying the knot at the back.

He picked up the sandals and examined their design. As a shoemaker, he appreciated their craftsmanship. They were made of several layers of tanned camel hide, cut in the shape of a sole, and the layers meticulously stitched together at the sides. The top was made of two broad straps of soft sheep leather stitched together in a Y shape and fastened to the sole on either side of the foot and on the inside of the big toe. There was also a separate strap of sheep leather to enclose the big toe itself. Kevork slipped them on his feet and wriggled his toes. They were sturdy, yet cool and comfortable.

Huda opened the tent flap and entered. Kevork saw her look him up and down, and then a huge grin appeared on her face. "No one would guess that you were Armenian," she said approvingly. She stepped up to him and adjusted the guttrah slightly. Then she led him out of the tent.

Kevork's eyes had become so accustomed to the dimness of the tent that the midday sun was like fire in his eyes. He squinted. There was a group of children wearing flowing Arabic robes playing tag. Several men were sitting together, talking languidly as they sipped tiny cups of coffee. A couple of women were cooking something in a big pot over an open fire. Another woman was gathering up camel dung to be used as fuel for the fire. The group resembled a relaxed and happy extended family.

Huda took him over to the group of men and waited silently until one, the eldest, deigned to notice her.

"Well Huda, I see that your *giaour* is alive and well."

"Yes, husband," replied Huda. "This is Khedive."

"Khedive?" said the husband. "A good Muslim name." Then he looked at Kevork carefully, noting the bearded face and the properly tied guttrah. To Kevork he said, "I will adopt you as my son if you prove worthy. Otherwise, you will have to leave."

Kevork swallowed hard, and nodded. "Thank you," he said.

"My name is Ibrahim Hassan, and I am the patriarch of this camp."

Kevork bowed in acknowledgment.

"And this is my eldest son, Aman. Consider him a brother."

One of the men who had been sitting and sipping coffee stood up and nodded his head in Kevork's direction. Kevork noticed that the man was really no more than a boy — perhaps his own age. Like Kevork, his face was bearded. But he was a hand shorter.

"Welcome to our home, brother," said Aman.

Kevork held out his hand, and Aman grasped it firmly. "Thank you," said Kevork.

The days and weeks passed in languid monotony.

Kevork did not feel like a terribly useful member of Ibrahim Hassan's household. He offered to make them sandals, but Ibrahim Hassan pointed out that they all had serviceable sandals, thank you very much. What else could be offer them?

Kevork was desperate to prove himself useful, and so when the old man suggested that he try keeping an eye on the camels as they grazed in the desert, he jumped at the chance. But he found it impossible to watch every one of the tall, gangly beasts. One would wander off in one direction, and another in the exact opposite direction.

Then Ibrahim Hassan explained. "Khedive, my son, you do not have to keep an eye on all the camels all the time. They are smart, and will make their way back to us eventually."

"But how do I get them to come in at the end of the day?"

"See that camel?" asked Ibrahim, and he pointed out one that didn't look any different to Kevork than all the rest. "That camel is the leader. Just watch over him. When it is time to round them up at night, jump on his back and lead him to our camp. The rest will follow."

Kevork grew to enjoy the camel duty. Being alone in the openness of the desert for long stretches during the day gave him time to reflect on all that had happened to him. He also used the time to get a bearing on exactly where he was in the vast desert. The Euphrates was half a day's walk away, and he knew that he could follow the river to Aneh, and Deir-Ez-Zor. Would it be possible to get all the way back to Marash? That was his dream.

The food at the encampment was plentiful, but not very interesting. The women would make a big vat of gooey white sorghum. Everyone would stand around the pot and scoop out bits using their fingers as spoons. It was a bland and monotonous diet, but Kevork was thankful for any food at all.

Kevork wasn't the only one in the encampment who found the gooey mush monotonous. One day, Ibrahim came up to him and said, "Khedive, my almost son. It is time for you to prove that you can earn your keep — you will help Aman steal a cow."

Kevork stared. "But stealing is wrong."

Ibrahim Hassan laughed out loud, but his eye held a glint of menace. "You're starting to sound like a *giaour* — an infidel."

"I will help my father steal a cow," Kevork said, swallowing hard. "I would do anything for my father."

The Arab grinned broadly.

"This is the plan," said Aman, Kevork's adoptive brother. "In the dead of night, we go over to the next encampment. They have many fine cows. I will find a nice fat one and tie a rope around its neck."

"What do you want me to do?" Kevork asked.

"You must stay close to me. Once I have found the right cow, you must twist its tail as I pull her forward."

"Twist the cow's tail? Are you serious?"

"Of course," said Aman. "Otherwise the cow won't budge. But twisting on its tail will distract it and it will walk forward."

Much to Kevork's surprise, the plan worked. When they got back to their own campsite, Kevork found that Ibrahim and the other men had dug a big hole in the ground and filled it with dried camel dung, and it was smoldering like charcoal. The cow was slaughtered, disembowelled, and lowered into the pit. Then the makeshift oven was covered up. The smell of roasting meat was delightful after so many weeks of sorghum goo.

The first bit of meat tasted heavenly. The desert clan feasted all night long, bellies bursting with contentment and faces glistening with fat. Every last trace of the cow disappeared.

"Kevork, you are truly worthy of being my son," said Ibrahim Hassan, the morning after the feast.

CHAPTER TWENTY-THREE

It was so boring and tedious at the haremlik that Mariam actually looked forward to Rustem's wedding festivities. At least it would be a break in the monotony. Ede was looking forward to it too, but for a different reason. "I cannot get married until Rustem does," she explained to Mariam.

Turkish weddings were quite different from anything Mariam had ever experienced, and Ede took it upon herself to explain the intricacies to Mariam. The men and the women stayed segregated throughout. Even the ceremony itself was performed without the bride.

For the women, the highlight of the wedding preparations was the *Gelin Hamami* — the Bride's Bath. The women from both the bride's and the groom's households were expected to attend, and that included Mariam.

Carriages of women arrived at the public bath on the appointed day. Guluzar Hanim had paid in advance to ensure that only the women of the bride's and groom's families were allowed to enter. She had sent her servants early to scrub everything down until the walls and floors shone bright and smelled faintly of lemon. She also arranged for platters of special delicacies to be delivered at specified intervals throughout the day.

Mariam and Ede arrived in one of Guluzar Hanim's first carriages, and then waited with anticipation for the arrival of the bride-to-be. When the first carriage of Halah Mustapha's household finally arrived, the women of Rustem Agha's household tittered in excitement.

Mariam watched as the carriage door opened. An older woman stepped out first. She reached in and grabbed the hand of a frightened-looking girl who looked no more than a child.

"She is very nice," whispered Ede to Mariam. "But shy."

Halah Mustapha wore the traditional bridal bath costume that had been delivered to her house from Rustem Bey's house a few days earlier. The costume consisted of a beautifully embroidered vest and a pair of loose felt trousers known as *shalvar*. Over top of this was a silk caftan, ankle length and open at the front. The cuffs and front border and bottom edges were embroidered with intricate geometric designs. Mariam thought that she looked like a child dressing up in her mother's clothing.

Halah walked towards the entrance of the bath, followed by a woman banging rhythmically on a drum. After the drummer came women from the Mustapha household. Ede grabbed Mariam's hand and they followed behind the other women.

The women cheered and chanted as Halah stepped into the bathhouse. She walked through the big reception area and was led to the cold room, where she removed all of her clothing behind a veil held by women in her family. Once she was naked, the women wrapped her in the veil and led her to a smaller warm room where a platform had been set up. Mariam noticed that the girl was flushed pink. Was it embarrassment or excitement? she wondered. Halah climbed onto the platform and sat down. The bath attendants came in and dumped buckets of hot water on her one at a time.

Halah was then asked to lie down, and one of her aunts scrubbed her skin with a coarse cloth until it glowed. Another member of her family washed her hair, all the while Ede, Mariam, and the other ladies in the room chanted and sang in rhythm with the beating of the drum.

Once the bathing was finished, Halah's mother came forward with a beautiful pair of high jewelled pattens. Halah sat up and put these on her feet, and then she was draped in the veil and led into the reception room.

A high throne-like chair had been set up for her, and her mother led her to it by the hand. She sat down, still wrapped in the veil, and then a henna artist came forward to decorate her hands and feet.

Mariam watched with fascination as the henna artist applied the mud-like substance to the girl's eyebrows, and then her hands. An attendant came forward with strips of cloth and carefully wrapped the girl's hands. When that was finished, the attendant removed the girl's pattens, and the muck was applied in intricate swirls to her feet. When that was finished, her feet were wrapped in strips of cloth. Throughout the procedure, Halah watched the henna artist with detached interest. It was as if the girl were watching henna being applied to someone else.

"Let us eat while the henna sets," announced Halah's mother.

Platters of food were brought in, and the guests helped themselves. Halah couldn't eat because her hands were wrapped up, so her mother chose some delicacies and put them on a plate and then sat by the girl's side and fed her. Halah took small bites and smiled gratefully at her mother.

The singing and eating lasted for several hours, and the henna artist checked under the strips of cloth from time to time to see if the henna had set. "It is ready," she announced finally.

An attendant brought a bowl of water and a cloth and unwrapped the girl's hands and feet. She carefully rubbed off every last bit of dried muck, and as she did, a beautifully intricate design of swirling red emerged on the girl's hands and feet. When the muck came off of her eyebrows, Halah looked older and more serious. Not so much a little girl.

"I can hardly wait until I get to wear the henna," said Ede.

Now came the time to put makeup on the bride, and so the makeup artist approached with her heavy bag of supplies. Mariam watched with fascination as Halah's face was covered with a luminous powder and her eyes were outlined with kohl. Her lips were lined with dark red paint and then filled in with a lighter red. The result was startling. Halah looked like a porcelain doll.

As if she were a doll and not a girl, Halah stood obediently as the women from her family dressed her back up in the vest and trousers and the beautifully embroidered caftan. She sat back down on the throne-like platform and candles were passed around to all the guests. With great solemnity, the candles were lit and one woman grabbed a tambourine. Halah stood up and followed the woman beating the tambourine. All of the other women lined up behind the bride, their candles lit. The women marched around the bathhouse pool behind the bride, singing songs and holding their candles high.

After several circuits around the pool, the bride's mother unfurled the wedding veil and covered her daughter's head with it. When Halah's head was covered, it was time for all the unmarried girls to throw coins into the pool and make their wishes. Mariam could hear Ede whisper her hope for a kind husband. What Mariam wished for was the safety of her family.

Halah walked out of the bathhouse to her waiting carriage. The woman with the drum and all of the other women followed, chanting as they marched. The carriage drove her back to her own house.

"Why isn't she going to the groom's house?" asked Mariam.

"She is not needed yet," answered Ede. "She will spend the rest of today and all of the night alone in a room. The men will hold the wedding ceremony and one of Halah's male relatives will act as her proxy.

When it is all over, the men from both families will come and get her."

Mariam didn't say it out loud, but she thought it very strange that a bride wouldn't be at her own wedding.

It wasn't until they got back to the haremlik that Mariam realized Ani hadn't been at the bathhouse, and she wasn't at the haremlik. She found Parantzim sound asleep with Rustem's two younger sisters, but Taline was missing, too. She looked in every room, and she scoured the garden, but Ani couldn't be found, and neither could Taline. On her way back in from the garden, she encountered Guluzar Hanim.

She bowed deeply, then asked, "Have you seen Ani?"

Guluzar Hanim hesitated, then answered. "Rustem Bey has sent Ani to Canada to be with her relatives. She took Taline with her."

"That's wonderful!" exclaimed Mariam. "I wonder why she didn't come to say goodbye to me first?"

After the wedding, Halah Hanim settled into the daily routine of the haremlik. As Rustem Bey's first wife, she held a senior position, so Guluzar Hanim kept her at her side and let her assist as Guluzar Hanim supervised the kitchen and the laundry and went over the food purchases for the week. Halah was also given a large private bedroom of her own, and as part of her wedding gift, Guluzar Hanim had it completely refurbished with a Western-style bed and dresser.

Mariam noticed that the girl was friendly to Ede and everyone else in the haremlik. Everyone but herself.

If only she would talk to me, thought Mariam. Then I could let her know she had nothing to be jealous about.

Deep down, Mariam knew that wasn't quite true. Each time she looked at Halah Hanim, she had an undeniable twinge of jealousy. Rustem Bey's private visits to Mariam stopped with his marriage. It surprised Mariam that she missed talking to him as much as she did.

One day, about six months after his marriage, he came upon Mariam as she was walking in circles in the garden. She was so intent in her own thoughts that she almost bumped into him as he stood in her path.

"Have you been well?" he asked, looking into her eyes.

"Well enough," replied Mariam. "It is kind of you to keep me here. And Parantzim too."

Rustem Bey nodded. "I know that you are anxious to leave, and soon you may be able to."

"What do you mean?" asked Mariam.

"The Turkish government has capitulated to the Allied forces."

Mariam gasped. She had been living in a vacuum for so many months that it was hard for her to grasp the implications. How wonderful it would be to leave this place. Perhaps find her sister.

"Are you so anxious to leave my house?" asked Rustem sadly. "I had hoped that you were happy here."

"You have been kind," said Mariam. "But I don't belong here." She was about to turn from him and continue her meditative walk, but then she added, "I have not had the opportunity to thank you."

"For what?" he asked.

"For sending Ani to live with her relatives in Canada. She was so sad here, after all. And to send Taline with her. It must have cost a fortune."

Rustem looked at her in confusion. "I did not send Ani and Taline to Canada."

"But your mother told me you did," replied Mariam.

Rustem paled. His mother was cold and calculating, and she always got what she wanted. "I ... I have to go," he said. And then he turned and walked away.

She was in her bedroom lying on the divan with a damp cloth over her eyes. Halah Hanim, plump with child, was sitting on a cushion at her feet, working intently on a piece of embroidery.

He didn't sit down and he said nothing to his wife. Instead, he stood in front of the divan with his hands on his hips. "What did you do with Ani and Taline?" he asked.

He saw a faint smile form on his mother's lips. "It took you long enough to notice," she said.

"What did you do with them?" he asked.

"Too many Armenians," said Guluzar Hanim. "I had them killed."

Rustem Bey swore under his breath. He walked out of her room without saying another word.

He walked back to the garden and grabbed Mariam by both arms. "You and Parantzim are leaving right now," he said. "Pack up your bags and I'll take you to the orphanage myself."

CHAPTER TWENTY-FOUR

While Kevork was happy to have gained Ibrahim Hassan's favour, he also realized that it meant he would soon have to leave. To fully be accepted as a son, Kevork would have to become a Muslim, and that was something he would never do. In addition to the religious ceremony, there was a physical requirement for all Muslim men: circumcision. It was the one physical difference between Christians and Muslims. Aside from the fact that Kevork did not relish the thought of having his privates operated on in a very public ceremony, he knew that if he went through with the circumcision, he truly would be leaving his heritage behind. If he ever found Marta again, what would she think of him?

Fortunately, the Maulvi Bakar, the spiritual leader of the clan, was away on an extended trip. Kevork would not have to act until he returned.

Not one bit of work was done at the camp on the

day after the feast; even the women spent the day relaxing and digesting their big meal.

That night, a man from the neighbouring camp came over to talk to Ibrahim.

"Did a cow wander down this way last night?" he asked diplomatically.

"No," replied Ibrahim with a belch and a smile. "We have seen no lost cow."

The man looked around and saw people resting on mats in the shade, round-bellied and greasy with contentment. Kevork watched as his eyes rested on the charred remnants of the barbecue pit, and his nose crinkled at the rich aroma of cooked meat that still hung in the air.

The man from the other camp frowned in annoyance and turned to leave. Ibrahim's expression softened. "I assure you," he said, "if a cow happens to wander off again, it will wander from another encampment, not yours."

The man's frown disappeared. "That is satisfactory," he said. And he left.

Kevork's long-term goal was to escape, but his short-term goal was to get clean. At the orphanage, he had grown accustomed to a weekly bath and periodic lice checks, but in the desert the lice ruled supreme. He was itchy all over, especially his eyes. Every morning when Kevork woke up, his eyes would be glued shut with mucus. He would have to use a bit of his precious drinking water just to unglue his eyelids each day. Kevork also longed for a bath, but he knew enough not to ask for a bath in the desert. Water was too precious a commodity to be wasted.

What surprised him was that others in the encampment didn't seem to be as bothered by the bugs as he was. It wasn't that they were more used to the lice, they just didn't seem to get them. One day, he asked Huda about this.

She looked at him in amused surprise. "Do you mean to tell me that you have been living with us all this time and you still don't know how we kill lice?"

He looked down at his feet in embarrassment.

"When you're out watching the camels," she said, "wait until the sun is directly overhead, and then take off your clothing and lay it out in the sun. The lice will fry up and die."

The next day, Kevork did just that, ensuring that he had a place in the shade to wait while his clothing baked in the sun.

"I am still covered with lice," he complained to Huda when he brought back the camels at the end of the day.

"They can't be coming from your clothing," she said, her brow creased in thought. "I should cut your hair."

She had him strip down to nothing but a piece of cloth around his waist and then she cut his hair. As it fell into the sand around him, lice skittered away. Kevork remembered when he was Kevork and he had cut Marta's hair. The memory made his heart ache.

"Now your beard," she said.

The dirty hair and beard blew away in tufts. Kevork started to feel like the person he used to be.

But he stayed Khedive for another year. He was treated just like Ibrahim Hassan's other son, Aman. And a year of fresh air and sorghum helped him grow strong. He longed to get back to Marash and reclaim his old life, but life as Ibrahim Hassan's son was so comfortable and secure that he kept putting it off. Then Maulvi Bakar came back.

"Khedive, my son," said Ibrahim Hassan. "We can now make your place in this family official. The Maulvi Bakar can perform the circumcision ritual and you shall be a full Muslim."

Kevork had no intention of being circumcised. Wearing Arab clothing and living like an Arab was reversible, but circumcision? That was for life.

He did not want to hurt Ibrahim, who had been so kind to him, but what could he do? The only thing to do was to buy himself a little bit of time and then think of some way to leave.

"Father," said Kevork as convincingly as he could, "it is my desire to be an obedient son. When will the circumcision take place?"

"Today," said Ibrahim Hassan with a smile. "The Maulvi Bakar is preparing himself for you now."

The time for dallying was gone. Kevork knew that he had to leave his adopted family immediately. But he couldn't leave without saying goodbye to Huda. He found her, standing at a distance from the encampment, gazing out at the desert.

"It's time for me to leave."

She turned to him with tears in her eyes. "I know, my son," she said. "You must live among your own people."

Kevork dried the tears from her cheek with the sleeve of his thwab. "Thank you for everything," he said. "You have been a mother to me."

Huda took one deep breath to control her sobs, and then she looked him in the eyes. "You must leave quickly," she said. "My husband will be deeply hurt when he realizes that you do not wish to be his son."

She hugged him fiercely for an instant, then pushed him away. She fumbled with the folds in her robe and pulled out a skin of water and a packet tied with a thin strip of cowhide. "Take these," she said. "Walk towards the setting sun." Huda pointed out the direction. "Aleppo is a week's walk away. It is a mostly Arab city, so the Armenians are safe. Perhaps you'll be able to build a life for yourself there."

He tried to give her one last hug, but she pushed his arms away. "Go," she said, her voice cracking with emotion. "Get out of here!" Then she turned and walked back to the encampment.

As he walked away from the group of desert wanderers, his mind was in a turmoil. "Am I mad? Leaving behind the security and anonymity of desert life and walking straight back into Turkey?"

He also felt guilty about deceiving his adopted father. Ibrahim Hassan had accepted him with open arms and had treated him exactly the same as if he had been his son by birth. But there was a difference, and Khedive — no, he was Kevork — Kevork knew the difference: Ibrahim Hassan only loved the lie. Kevork could not live the rest of his life pretending to be someone else. Better to die an Armenian than live a lie.

Kevork also had the slim hope that Marta was still living. Seeing Huda alive and well after decades of Muslim life also gave him hope that Mariam still lived, that perhaps even his mother was still alive and he might find her one day. But he would never be able to find any of them if his own identity was hidden.

When he was several hours away from the encampment, Kevork sat down for a few minutes' rest. He took a tiny sip of water, then opened the packet Huda had given him. She had filled it with thin strips of sun-dried beef — a precious treasure indeed!

There was a small swatch of brightly coloured cloth tied in a knot. He opened it. A gold coin. All of the gold coins that had been sewn into Kevork's clothing had disappeared during the deportation. Kevork looked at this one carefully and realized that it was very old. Huda must have hoarded this away as her one piece of security. A sob caught in Kevork's throat. It was an incredible act of generosity.

Kevork walked through the desert all the way to Aleppo. He was terrified of being recognized as an Armenian and deported again, but the groups he passed seemed not to notice him. With his sun-darkened skin and his thwab and guttrah, he was given free passage.

Within a week, he stood at the gates of Aleppo.

Chapter Twenty-Five

"I won't go!" screamed Parantzim. "This is my home."

Mariam sat down on the floor beside the little girl and pulled her to her lap. "I am your mother now, and your home is with me," she said.

"I like it here," said Parantzim. "There is food and beautiful clothing. And if I have to go, why do Ayesha and Leyla get to stay?"

Mariam wiped the angry tears from Parantzim's face with the cuff of her robe and then she whispered into the little girl's ear, "It is not safe here anymore."

"That is a lie," said Parantzim. "I love it here."

Mariam looped one arm under the girl's legs and another around her back, and then she struggled to stand. Parantzim was heavier than she realized, and they both fell down. "Why are you taking me away like this? It is not fair," the girl wailed.

Rustem Bey appeared at the door. He looked down

on the floor at Mariam sprawled out with Parantzim. "Let me help you," he said.

He lifted Parantzim up with a single arm, then extended his free hand to help Mariam to her feet. "Come," he said. "The carriage is ready."

He walked quickly through the corridor towards the front entrance. Ede Kadin stood in the hallway, her mouth half-open with surprise. "I'll explain later," said Rustem Bey, as he walked past her with the flailing girl over his shoulder and Mariam at his side.

When they stepped out into the sunlight, Mariam automatically covered her face with a yashmak. She realized that she didn't have to do that anymore. She was free! But somehow, she'd feel funny being outside without it on.

Rustem put Parantzim in the carriage first, and then he helped Mariam with the step. He looked in confusion at the ground once Mariam was sitting inside the carriage. "Where is your bundle of clothing?" he asked.

"I came here with nothing," said Mariam, "and I will leave the same way."

"But you're welcome to the clothing I had made for you," said Rustem Bey, a hurt look on his face.

"Thank you," said Mariam. "You are very generous. You always have been. But I wish to leave it behind."

"I don't," interjected Parantzim weepily. "If I have to leave, I want to take my pretty clothing."

"You'll have no need for it at the orphanage," said Mariam firmly. "Now please be quiet."

Rustem Bey told the driver where they were going, and then he hopped into the carriage and sat across from Mariam. He didn't want to talk about what had happened to Ani and Taline in front of Parantzim, but he could see how shaken Mariam was.

"I am sorry about the girls," he said.

Mariam looked up and met his eyes. They were filled with tears. "I appreciate all you have done," she said.

They rode the rest of the distance in silence.

When the carriage passed through the orphanage gates, Mariam held her yashmak to her face and peeked out the carriage window. She saw that the grounds were again filling with children. So many orphans. It made her heart ache.

The carriage pulled up just outside of Miss Younger's office, and Rustem stepped down first. He held out his hand and helped Mariam down.

A group of ragged boys ran past just at that moment, and they looked at Rustem Bey, and then at Mariam and Parantzim.

"Turkish murderers!" one of them yelled. Another picked up a stone and threw it, hitting Parantzim on the side of the head as she stepped down. Parantzim screamed, then clung to Rustem Bey. "Please don't leave me here," she wailed.

Rustem reached down and picked Parantzim up. He nuzzled his face in her hair and swallowed back a sob. "Listen to your mother," he said. He gave her one last hug, then set her down on the ground beside Mariam.

Mariam grabbed Parantzim's hand and whispered, "I am doing this for you."

Just then, the door of the office opened, but it wasn't Miss Younger who stepped out. It was a monocled man with a starched white shirt rolled up to the elbows.

"Hello, hello!" he said, holding out his hand in welcome.

Mariam stood quietly by Rustem's side, holding Parantzim protectively in front of her.

The man peered into Mariam's eyes above the yashmak. "You've been living with a Turk and now you and your daughter want to be Armenian again, is that right?"

Mariam nodded. Where was Miss Younger? she wondered.

"Thanks, good fellow," said the man to Rustem. "It was good of you to bring them."

The man started to lead Mariam by the elbow, but she stopped. She walked over to Rustem and lifted her yashmak, then stood on tiptoes and kissed him on the cheek. "You are a true friend," she said. "Thank you."

Rustem Bey was nearly overcome with tears, and he didn't want Mariam to see that, so he turned brusquely away and walked back to the carriage.

"Let us go," said the man to Mariam.

She followed him. "My name is Mr. Brighton," he said. "I've come from America."

What could she say?

He led Mariam and Parantzim to a building that used to be one of the dormitories for the female missionaries. "This is the Rescue Home for Women," said Mr. Brighton.

Mariam still said nothing.

Mr. Brighton continued. "You must learn to abandon Turkish ways. When you emerge, you'll be fully

Armenian. If we let you out with the orphans and surviving adults the way you are, you'd be ostracized."

Mariam nodded. Now she was one of *Them*.

He held the door open for her, and she and
Parantzim stepped through. It was furnished just like
her dormitory room of old with a row of simple beds
and a table at one end with a pitcher of water. There
was a window at the far end of the room, and a woman
sat there, looking out the window. She wore a Turkish
housedress, and Mariam could tell by looking at the
outline of her back that she was heavy with child. The
woman turned when she heard the door click shut.

Mariam gasped. It was her sister, Marta.

CHAPTER TWENTY-SIX

Kevork stayed on in Aleppo. There was a dire need for shoemakers in this Arab city, and there were no Turks on the hunt for Armenians. Just to be safe, Kevork kept with his adopted Arab-style of dress. But he used his real name, in the hopes that Marta or Mariam would somehow find him.

As he walked through the bazaar to his booth each morning, Kevork listened to the buzz of gossip. When Turkey lost the war, his heart skipped a beat. Would it be safe to travel back to Marash? If only he knew.

And what he really wanted to know was if Marta lived. In his heart, he felt that she was still alive. But where was she, and how could he find her? The orphanage called to him like a beacon, but he had to wait until the time was right.

Most of what Kevork made in his shop were sandals in the Arabic style. He had become quite proficient at them. But one day a foreigner came in, bearing a Turkish-English dictionary and a strange request.

"Boots," said the man, struggling with his Turkish.

Boots in the desert? wondered Kevork. It brought back memories.

He flipped through his dictionary once again. "Mountain," said the man.

Boots? Mountain? What was he talking about?

The man pointed to his feet, then mimicked walking up a hill with exaggerated motions.

"Marash ... mountains ... walk ... walk," said the man. Marash?

All at once, Kevork knew who this man was. Just the day before, Kevork had been sipping coffee with one of his friends when he had heard about this man. He was Leslie Davis, the new consulate from America. Unlike other government officials who travelled everywhere with a whole entourage, this Leslie Davis walked all over the place: up hills and mountains, through the desert, through back streets. He did this without servants or a carriage and was considered quite mad.

Kevork nodded enthusiastically. Boots? Yes!

"Marash," said Kevork, pointing to his chest. "Me, from Marash."

The American frowned, not understanding.

Then Kevork took a chance. "Me Armenian," he said.

Leslie Davis nodded in understanding. "You, me, Marash together."

Kevork grinned broadly. He was that much closer to Marta.

ACKNOWLEDGEMENTS

I would like to thank Arsho Zakarian, who opened her heart, her mind, and her books to me. The fine details of Armenian and Turkish life would not have been possible without her assistance. Sincere thanks to Carl Georgian, whose stories of his father Kevork Kevorkian (George Georgian) were the inspiration for my character, Kevork. The late Aram Aivaizian was also instrumental in making this book possible. His stories of being an orphan after the massacres were vivid and crisp. Aram also loaned me dozens of books and read early drafts of my manuscripts. Sincere thanks also to Linda Eley and Denise Kirk of the Brantford Public Library, who provided me with materials for this novel via inter-library loan. Sincere thanks to Herminé Najarian who took me into her home and cooked up an Armenian feast and told me stories of her father's survival from the massacres. Also, a big thank you to Rosdom Yeghoyan, who clarified many small cultural details for me. Hugs and thanks to Mom and Bill for their speedy reading and eagle eyes.

A big hug to my husband, Orest, who helped me out of more computer glitches than I care to admit. I would also like to thank the private kidcritters in Compuserve's Litforum. The timely and pertinent feedback from Polly Martin, Kate Coombs, Karen Dyer, Linda Gerber, Julie Kentner, Sheryl Toy, Lori Benton, Janet McConnaughey, Merrill Cornish, Linda Mikolayenko, and Rosemarie Reichel saved me much time and hair-pulling. I would also like to thank Natalia Buchok, Eliz Sharabkhanian, and Houri Najarian, who all read the completed manuscript and offered corrections for cultural accuracy. Sincere thanks to Dr. David Jenkinson, whose encouragement convinced me to try my hand at writing a novel set entirely in the past.

This novel would not have been possible without the encouragement and patience of my agent, Dean Cooke, and his assistant, Samantha North. I would also like to thank my editor, Barry Jowett, for his sharp eye and kind words.